What did a goddess's kisses taste like?

"Let's see," Travis said, his eyes skimming along the contours of her face, "we've discussed kids and marriage, all before we've even kissed." Was it his imagination, or did his throat tighten just a wee bit as he made his observation?

All the butterflies in Shana's stomach lined up on the runway, bracing for take-off, then glided off into the horizon in unison as she drew her courage to her, draping it about herself like a blanket. Or a protective shield.

"There's an easy solution for that," she told him, then congratulated herself that her voice didn't crack or tremble.

One arched eyebrow raised itself. "Oh?"

"Yes, 'oh.'"

And then, before she lost her nerve, Shana leaned over into his space. Framing his face with her long, delicate fingers, she pressed her lips against his....

Dear Reader,

Well, here we are, watching the fourth of Kate's boys go down as Cupid's arrows finally find him. Workaholic Travis Marlowe was the son who became a lawyer and secretly felt, with one broken engagement behind him, that love was not a playing field he could successfully navigate. But this was before Shana O'Reilly brought her father to him in order to draft a living trust. Before Travis knows it, he's back burning the midnight oil, but this time, work has very little to do with it. Yet loving someone is never as easy as it should be, especially when his client shares a secret with him about Shana that could completely devastate her life. A secret Travis is not free to share with her.

I hope you enjoy this latest installment of KATE'S BOYS. It was supposed to be the last of the series, but as you probably already know, I do have a problem with letting go. And, after all, Kate and Bryan did also have a daughter....

As ever, I thank you for reading, and from the bottom of my heart, I wish you someone to love who loves you back.

With affection,

Marie Ferrarella

MARIE FERRARELLA

TRAVIS'S APPEAL

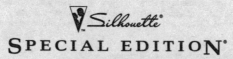

SPECIAL EDITION®

Published by Silhouette Books

America's Publisher of Contemporary Romance

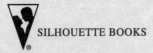

SILHOUETTE BOOKS

ISBN-13: 978-0-373-65440-6
ISBN-10:   0-373-65440-5

Recycling programs
for this product may
not exist in your area.

TRAVIS'S APPEAL

MARIE FERRARELLA

This *USA TODAY* bestselling and RITA® Award-winning author has written more than one hundred and fifty novels for Silhouette Books, some under the name Marie Nicole. Her romances are beloved by fans worldwide. Visit her Web site at www.marieferrarella.com.

To
Evelyn,
And the Ghost
Of Christmas Past

Chapter 1

It was another typical day in paradise.

While the carefully made-up newscasters talked about "storm watches" and blizzards hitting every state both east and north of New Mexico, here, in Bedford, happily nestled in the middle of Southern California, the sun was seductively caressing its citizens with warm, loving fingers.

Travis Marlowe would have preferred rain. He wished for a gloomy, rainy day where the sun absented itself and illumination came from artificial sources rather than the incredibly bright orb in the sky.

Rain and gloom would have far better suited his current mood. Moreover, the lack of light would have soothed his present condition. He had no idea why his head hadn't killed him yet.

It was true what they said. No good deed went unpunished.

All right, it wasn't exactly a good deed. It was part of his job. Kind of. While the firm's bylaws didn't state that burning the midnight oil was part of the job, he still felt it was required—even if he was the only one doing the requiring.

Angry little devils with sledgehammers pounded along the perimeter of his temples.

That's what he got for staying up most of the night, working out the kinks in Thomas Fielder's revocable living trust and then deciding to sack out on the sofa in his office rather than driving home at almost five in the morning.

The firm, leather sofa, while perfectly fine for sitting, was definitely not the last word in comfort for sleeping. Not only his head, but his neck ached, thanks to the rather strange position he'd woken up in this morning. His neck felt not unlike a pipe cleaner permanently bent out of shape.

To add insult to injury, every time he turned his head, horrible pains shot out of nowhere, piercing the base of his neck and making Travis wish that he'd died sometime in the early morning.

But here it was, a brand new *sunny* day and he had to face it. And look relatively happy about it.

Taking the change of shirt and underwear he kept in the bottom drawer for just such an emergency, Travis hoped that a quick shower in the executive bathroom would help set him back on the right track.

"Go home," his father, one of the senior partners for the family law firm where he worked, said by way of a greeting. A quick assessment had Bryan adding, "You really look like hell."

Bryan Marlowe made no secret of the fact that he was quite happy that at least one of his four sons had followed him into law. Not a man to brag, it was still very obvious that he was proud of his son. Travis thought, if his father was telling him to go home, he must look like death warmed over—or a reasonable facsimile thereof.

"I'll look better after a quick shower," Travis promised. He was about to nod at the clothing in his arms, but stopped himself—and prevented another onslaught of pain—just in time.

Bryan snorted as his eyes traveled the length of his son. "That will be one hell of a rejuvenating shower." Pausing, Bryan frowned. "Why didn't you go home last night like everyone else?" he asked.

Travis shrugged, his broad shoulders moving beneath a light blue dress shirt in desperate need of an iron. "You know how it is. You keep telling yourself 'Oh, just one more thing'…and then, suddenly, it's morning. Or close to it."

Somewhere on the floor honeycombed with suites, one of the attorneys slammed a door. The sound reverberated throughout the hall. Travis winced as the sound ground its heel into his head.

"Headache?" Bryan guessed.

There was no point in lying. "Yeah. A doozy."

The answer just reinforced Bryan's initial reaction. "Like I said, go home, Travis. Take a personal day and take that shower in your own bathroom."

Travis had no desire to go home, where time hung too heavily on his hands. "I'm fine, really. Besides, never know when I might need one of those personal days. Better to save them."

Bryan frowned. He had a case he wanted to review before his early morning appointment arrived, but as his wife Kate had taught him, nothing was more important than family. And right now, that meant Travis.

"I wish to God you needed to take one of those personal days. You know, Travis, when you told me that you wanted to go into family law, I don't think there was a prouder father under the sun. I mean, I love all of you boys—and Kelsey," Bryan tossed in his daughter's name. Because she was the last born, and a girl, he had a tendency to place her in a category all her own, something Kelsey bristled at when he did. "And I'm proud of each of you, but I'd be lying if I didn't say I was a little disappointed when Mike, Trevor and Trent didn't follow me into the field. I always envisioned all five of us having our own company."

The corners of Travis's mouth curved. "Marlowe and Sons?"

"Something like that," Bryan freely admitted. "Still, one is better than none and your brothers all have done very well in their chosen fields."

Travis was vaguely aware that he had someone coming in this morning, although the exact time escaped him. He needed to get ready. "Where's this going, Dad?"

Bryan stopped, amused rather than annoyed at the prodding. "We're lawyers, Travis. Roundabout is our regular route."

Travis smiled indulgently. "Sorry."

"My point," Bryan confided, "is that you turned out to be more like me than I ever thought possible."

Travis studied his father's face. It was a face that, if he so desired, gave nothing away. "That's a compliment, right?"

"Yes and no," Bryan allowed. "Your dedication is admirable. The fact that you do nothing else *but* work is not." Here, his son had turned out to be too much like him. The *old* him, Bryan amended silently. Because he was familiar with the signs, he wanted to help his son avoid the pitfalls. "Now, I know exactly how easy it is to get caught up in things because it's easier to do that than face your own problems. Until Kate came along and pointed it out, I didn't even realize I was doing that."

He and his brothers were well aware of the significant changes his stepmother had brought into all their lives. She arrived and took over the duties that three other nannies had fled from in quick succession. Still, he didn't want his father extrapolating that into his own life.

"I'm not working because I don't want to face any problems, Dad," Travis insisted. "I'm working because I like working."

"It cost you Adrianne," Bryan reminded his son quietly.

Travis paused and took a breath. Adrianne and he had

been engaged for approximately two months—until she'd thrown the ring at him. "Adrianne and I weren't a match. I'm lucky it ended the way it did. I actually dodged a bullet." Better to break up before a wedding than after one.

Bryan thought of it from his son's fiancée's point of view. Living with Kate had taught him to see things from perspectives other than his own. "It would have been easy enough for a bullet to find you. You were always at your desk—or in court."

Travis didn't want to talk about the issue. It was in the past and just reinforced his initial feelings about relationships. Very few turned out and they weren't worth the risk.

"Dad, things usually work out for the best. We weren't right for each other. According to the grapevine, Adrianne's with some guy now who can give her all the attention she wants."

Travis was more his son than the boy realized, Bryan thought.

"You know, after your mother died," Bryan said, referring to Jill, his first wife and the biological mother of his four sons, "I tried to bury myself in my work because I felt guilty. Guilty that I was alive when she wasn't, guilty that there might have been something I could have done to save her, to keep her from going on that trip. And I was afraid to commit to anyone else— even you boys—for fear of feeling that awful, awful pain of being abandoned again. It took Kate to make me see that loving someone, leaving yourself open to love, was worth every risk you can take."

Travis began to nod his head and stopped abruptly

when the motion sent a dozen arrows flying to his temples. This was going to be one hell of a day, he thought. Still, he dug in stubbornly.

"I'll keep that in mind," Travis promised. "Now, I really would like to take that shower."

Bryan stepped to the side, out of his son's way. "Turn the hot water all the way up. The steam might help your head."

"Gotcha," Travis said, heading toward the executive shower.

Not about to get into another discussion, Travis was just humoring his father. He knew from experience that with these headaches, the only thing that could help immediately was if someone gave him a new head. Short of that, it was a storm he just needed to ride out. Preferably in a room where the blinds were drawn.

Reaching the executive bathroom, Travis locked the door behind him and quickly stripped off his clothes. It took him less than a minute to adjust the water temperature. In the stall, he sighed, allowing the water to hit his back full force.

He appreciated his father's concern about the direction his life was taking, he really did, and in the privacy of his own mind, he might be willing to acknowledge a germ of truth in his father's supposition that he had a phobia about commitments. He was even willing to concede that it might be remotely rooted in his mother's demise.

But he really did like his work a great deal and Adrianne, it turned out, just liked the prestige of saying that her significant other, soon-to-be-husband, was a lawyer. Not that Adrianne wanted him doing any lawyering on her time, and her time was anytime she decided she needed to see him.

He was better off without her. When he saw his brothers, who had all paired up this last year, if he felt a little isolated, like the odd man out, he gave no indication. He was happy for his brothers, happy each had apparently found the one person who completed their world.

But for him, it wouldn't be that easy. Not because he wasn't looking but because he felt it was far too early to be thinking of being with someone on a permanent basis. Someone who, if the whim hit, could leave. Granted, Adrianne had turned out to be an unfortunate choice, but she just proved his theory. He was better off on his own. Better off working, doing what he was good at.

But analyzing deep-rooted feelings and subconscious ones, that was Trent's domain, not his. Trent was a child psychologist, like Kate. Trent was accustomed to multilayered thinking and digging deep. Travis liked things to be in black and white.

Like the law.

Travis stood beneath the showerhead a bit longer, letting the hot water hit him and the steam build up within the black, onyx-tiled stall. Slowly, some of the tension began to leave his shoulders. It helped. A tiny bit.

He got out before he turned pruney.

"Your hair's damp."

Travis's secretary, Bea Bennett, made the note. A small, thin, angular woman, she favored long skirts, sensible shoes and long, penetrating looks in lieu of arguing with her boss. She stepped into his office not ten minutes after he'd returned to it himself.

"The hair dryer died," Travis told her.

The device had given up the ghost midway through drying his sandy blond hair, making it appear a little darker. With the hair dryer refusing to rise up from the dead, he'd run his fingers through his hair a couple of times, getting rid of any excess water. Travis figured the air would take care of the rest eventually.

Thin, carefully penciled-in eyebrows rose in mild surprise. "The one in the executive bathroom?"

About to nod, Travis refrained. The headache was still very much a part of him, the tiny respite in the shower a thing of the past the moment he stepped away from the hazy warmth of the stall.

"That's the one."

Bea frowned, shaking her head, a head mistress trying to decipher the mystery that was her student. "Don't know what you people do with them. The one I've got at home's lasted going on seven years now."

Like everyone else at the firm, Travis was accustomed to the woman's outspoken manner. Most of the time, he actually got a kick out of it. This was not one of those times. Migraine headaches made him less tolerant of eccentricities.

"Good for you, Bea." He dug into his side drawer for the bottle of extra-strength aspirin. The aspirin that was powerless to relieve his headache. He took a couple of pills anyway. He had heard that if you believed something worked, it helped. He did his best to believe. Swallowing, he continued talking to her. "Now, did you come in here for a reason, Bea, or did you just want to bedevil me with your rapier wit and your arousing physical presence?"

Bea narrowed her eyes until the black marbles disappeared behind tiny slits. He didn't know if she was doing it for effect, or if she was myopic.

"When I'm bedeviling you, Mr. Marlowe, you won't have to ask if that's what I'm doing. You'll know it," the woman informed him. Then, with a toss of her head, she switched persona, becoming the perennial secretary. "Your ten o'clock appointment is here."

His ten o'clock. For a second, Travis drew a blank. He glanced at his calendar. He'd written a name beside the ten o'clock space, but it was now completely illegible to him.

"And he would be?" he asked, leaving the rest up in the air, waiting for Bea to fill in the blank.

"They," Bea corrected. "And they're outside in the reception area." She gestured behind her toward the common area where all but the most elite of the firm's clients waited.

Travis looked at the calendar again. It made less sense to him than before. He was really going to have to do something about his handwriting. "I need a name, Bea."

She eyed him, a small, thin face behind dark-rimmed glasses someone had once said she wore for effect rather than necessity. "Any particular one?" she asked glibly.

They were going to play the game her way, or not at all, Travis thought. Again, he might have enjoyed it if not for the civil war going on right behind his eyes. "The potential client's would be nice."

She crossed to his desk and made a show of examining his calendar. "What the hell is that?" she asked, pointing to the writing beside the number "10." "It looks like you dipped a chicken in ink and had it walk across your page." She looked at him again. "Didn't your parents teach you how to write?"

"They had more important things to teach me," he told her lightly. "Like how to fire an insubordinate secretary."

With a haughty little noise, she informed him, "I can't be fired."

His sense of humor was valiantly trying to claw its way back among the living. He was game. "And why's that?"

He fully expected her to say something about having tenure, since she had worked here longer than anyone could remember. But then, since this was Bea, he realized he should have known better. Conventional arguments were not for her.

"Slaves have to be sold," she informed him with a smart toss of her head. "And their name's O'Reilly." Bea paused to tap the calendar, as if that could somehow transform his handwriting into legible letters. "Shawn and Shana," she added.

"Married couple?" he guessed absently. The borders of family law were wide, taking in a myriad of subjects. There were twelve attorneys in the firm, each with a specialty although their work did encompass many fields within the heading.

A short laugh escaped like a burst of air. "Not

hardly," she cackled before becoming serious again. "Not unless the old man's into cradle robbing." She considered her own observation and commented on it. "'Course, a man with money these days thinks he could buy himself anything he wants."

"How about a secretary who doesn't give her own narrative to everything?" Travis suggested with a touch of wistfulness.

"Too boring." A wave of the hand accompanied her dismissive shake of the head. Her eyes swept over his desk just before she crossed to the doorway again. "By the way, those'll burn a hole in your stomach," she told him with a disapproving frown, referring to the bottle of extra-strength aspirin on his desk. "If you went home at a decent hour, like everyone else around here, maybe you wouldn't get those damn headaches of yours."

Bea knew everything that was going on in the office. She was better than a private investigator. He returned the bottle to the side drawer.

"I had no idea you cared, Bea."

Bea paused in the doorway to smile at him over her shoulder. "Always said you were clueless," she murmured before crossing the threshold. And then she stopped, turning around again. "By the way..."

The phrase hung in midair like one half of the old popular "shave and a haircut, two bits" refrain tapped out with knuckles hitting a hard surface. He gave in after less than a minute.

"What?" Travis prompted.

"Hang on to your socks."

He blinked. "What?" he demanded.

Rather than elaborate, Bea merely smiled at him. Her eyes danced with delight over her enigma. "You'll understand," she promised.

With that, she left the room.

In her wake, half a beat later, Travis's latest clients entered. His ten o'clock appointment, Shawn O'Reilly and Shana O'Reilly.

And Bea was right. Travis could feel his socks suddenly slipping down his ankles. Curling. Along with the hairs along his neck.

Shawn O'Reilly looked like a modern, slightly worn-out and pale version of a department store Santa Claus. But it was the young woman beside him, Shana, that Travis instinctively knew Bea had issued her warning about. Shana O'Reilly looked like something Santa Claus might have left beneath the Christmas tree of a deserving male if the latter had been exceptionally good, not just for the year, but for the sum total of his entire life.

Chapter 2

Travis stopped breathing.

To his recollection—and he was blessed with a mind that forgot absolutely *nothing*—Travis had never seen a more beautiful woman in his life. She was tall—about five-seven—slender, with the face of an angel and long, straight blond hair that brought to mind the phrase "spun gold." Her eyes were crystal-blue, and she moved like whispered poetry as she crossed the room.

Belatedly, Travis remembered that he was endowed with a rather pleasant, articulate voice and that remaining silently frozen in place like a plaster statue in an abandoned corner of a museum did not go a long way in inspiring confidence in clients.

Mentally shaking off his trance, Travis rose to his

feet. Rounding his desk, he paid for the quick action with another breath-snatching salvo of sharp pain firing across his temples.

Travis silently congratulated himself for not wincing. It would have made for a terrible first impression. People didn't expect their potential lawyer to wince when he first met them. At the very least, it would have conjured up a myriad of questions over his abilities.

"Hello." Putting on his widest smile, Travis extended his hand to the heavyset man. "I'm Travis Marlowe."

"Shawn O'Reilly," the man responded genially, then nodded his head toward the ray of sunshine on his right. "And this is Shana. O'Reilly," he added the surname as if it was an afterthought, then followed it up with, "My daughter." He actually beamed as he made the announcement.

Not that the man probably hadn't been a decent-looking sort in his youth, a hundred pounds and several chins ago, but this was definitely a case of the apple falling miles away from the tree. He and his brothers looked like a composite of their late mother and their father, while his sister, Kelsey, looked like a miniature version of Kate. Travis was fairly certain that Shana O'Reilly had to take after her mother because, other than the bright, cheerful, electric blue eyes, not a thing about her even remotely brought Shawn O'Reilly to mind.

"Hello," Shana said, extending her hand to him.

She had a voice like a low blues melody, sinfully seductive.

No surprise there. It took Travis a second to take her hand and shake it. Holding her hand, he experienced an almost overwhelming reluctance to release it again.

What the hell was going on with him, he silently upbraided himself. He was too young to be going through a second adolescence and too old to be going through his first one.

They were right, he concluded, those people who said that you weren't at your best without a full night's sleep. He was obviously not operating with all four engines burning.

Out of the corner of his eye, Travis saw Shana's father glancing toward one of the two chairs positioned in front of his desk. Shawn O'Reilly looked like a man trying to decide whether the chair would accommodate his girth without mishap or groaning, or the sofa would be a wiser course to follow.

Travis nodded toward the sofa. "You might find the sofa a bit more comfortable, Mr. O'Reilly," he suggested. "I know I do."

His words brought out an even wider smile from Shana. His breath went missing for a full thirty seconds. It was like standing beside an early morning sunrise.

Travis glanced down at her left hand. No ring.

Sunshine permeated his inner core.

Pleased at the suggestion, Shawn turned around and sat down on the sofa. Soft tan leather sighed all around the man's considerable form. Shana took a seat beside him, shifted slightly and crossed her legs, her white skirt hugging her thighs. Travis forced himself to look away. He wouldn't be able to form a coherent thought for several minutes if he didn't.

Grabbing one of the two chairs that stood facing his desk, he swung it around and sat down opposite his potential clients. A small, glass-topped coffee table took up the space between them.

"Can I get you anything?" Travis asked amiably, looking from the man to his daughter. "Coffee? Tea? Soda? Water?"

"We're fine," Shawn assured him.

"All right, then tell me," Travis settled back in his chair. "How can I help you?"

Shawn moved forward a touch, creating an aura of privacy as he did so. "They tell me you're the go-to guy around here when it comes to putting together a living trust."

Each at the firm had an area of expertise, although areas did overlap. Several attorneys specialized in living trusts. Somewhere, he had a guardian angel who had brought these people to him. "I've written a number of them, yes."

His answer seemed to irritate Shawn rather than please him. Shaggy gray eyebrows came together like teddy bear hamsters huddling for warmth. "I don't want false modesty, boy. I want the best."

All right, you want confidence, you'll get confidence. "Then you came to the right place," Travis told him.

A pleased smile folded itself into the ample cheeks. "Better," Shawn nodded. "A man should always know what he's capable of and what his shortcomings are."

Shawn's voice was big and booming, with a slight Texas flavor. The man was obviously not a native Californian.

Travis found himself wishing that his new client's tone was a little softer. Each word the man uttered seemed to vibrate inside his head which had turned into a living echo chamber.

Leaning forward, his elbows digging into his wide lap, Shawn asked without preamble, "Do these things really do what they say they do?"

He had no idea what the man referred to. It was a completely ambiguous question and Travis felt his way around slowly, not wanting to give offense or make Shawn think he was stupid. "And what is it that 'they' say, Mr. O'Reilly?"

"That if my money and my property are secured within the specifications of a living trust, then my girls won't have to go through probate or pay Estate taxes." When Shawn frowned, his chins became more prominent. "Already paid taxes on all the money once. Doesn't seem fair to have to pay taxes on it again just because my girls get to hang on to it instead of me when I die."

He heard that sentiment expressed a lot. Travis smiled. The effort cost him. It seemed that every movement, partial or otherwise, had pain associated with it. The aspirin he'd swallowed was taking its sweet time.

"That's why most people look into getting a living trust," he told Shawn.

The man nodded, pleased. "Now, we're not going

to be talking fortunes, boy. I'm not a Rockefeller," Shawn warned.

"Most people aren't," Travis acknowledged. "You mentioned your 'girls.' Spouses enjoy the greatest elimination or postponement of Estate Taxes. Other generations, less. But I'll need to know more about your particular assets and beneficiaries, after applying the Estate Tax Credit." His eyes shifted toward Shana. It didn't appear as if they were waiting for someone else to join them. That meant that Shana was the one the man relied on, Travis surmised. Beautiful and reliable. A hell of a combination. "I take it you're referring to your daughters."

"Well, yeah," Shawn laughed heartily. "I don't own no night club with dancing girls in it. Just a restaurant." The way he said it, Travis could tell that there was no "just" about it. "Been running it for longer than Shana's been on this earth," the man said proudly. "Want that to go into the living trust, too." Shawn pinned him with a look. "You can do that, right?"

"With the right wording, Mr. O'Reilly, I can include just about anything in that trust," Travis assured him. "Provided I have the proper documentation." He couldn't help wondering how open the man was to having a stranger go through his things. He sounded friendly enough, but privacy was an issue for some, despite the lawyer-client privilege so frequently cited.

Shawn cocked his head. Travis was reminded of an old painting he saw where Santa Claus was studying a list, deciding who was naughty or nice. "You mean like ownership papers?"

Travis nodded and instantly regretted it. "Those—" he said with a vain effort to will back the pain "—and the deed to your house as well as all your banking information. I'm going to need to review all of that if you want it to be covered in the trust."

"Hell, yes I want it covered," Shawn informed him with feeling. "Otherwise, there's no reason to be going through this, is there?" He cleared his throat. "No offense, but lawyers aren't exactly my favorite kind of people."

"None taken," Travis murmured. He heard that a lot, too. His headache was at the point where it could become blinding at any second. He needed more aspirin. "If you'll excuse me for a second."

Getting up, he saw Shawn and Shana exchange glances but couldn't guess at what they might be thinking. He needed a clear head for that, or at least one that didn't feel as if it were splintering into a million pieces.

Travis crossed back to his desk, took out the bottle of aspirin and shook out another two tablets. He downed them with the now cold cup of coffee that was standing, neglected, on his desk.

When he turned around again, he noticed Shawn eyeing him curiously.

"Too much partying last night?" the man guessed genially.

The expression on Shana's face belonged to that of a mother whose child had suddenly misbehaved.

"Dad, that is none of our business," she reprimanded softly.

"If he's gonna be my lawyer, it is," Shawn insisted, but his tone wasn't judgmental. He turned inquisitive blue eyes on Travis.

"Too many writs," Travis corrected, turning his words back around on him, and returning to his seat.

Shawn's eyes narrowed beneath his deep gray eyebrows. "Too many what?"

"I worked late," Travis explained. "I wound up catching a catnap on the sofa. It really wasn't made for sleeping."

The older man studied him. "You do that often? Work late?"

Travis couldn't gauge if that worked in his favor or not. The man's expression was unreadable.

"If something needs to be finished," Travis told him without fanfare. "I don't like falling behind." The latter sentence dribbled from his lips as he tried to follow Shana's movements. She'd risen from the sofa and was now circling behind him. "Can I help you?" he asked. Twisting around to look at her sent another set of arrows through his temples.

"No," she answered simply. "But I think I might be able to help you."

"I don't—"

He was about to say that he didn't understand what she meant, but the final words never materialized. They stopped, mid-flow, drying up on his lips as he felt her fingertips delicately touch the corners of his temples. Ever so gently, she slowly began to make small, concentric circles along his skin, pressing just enough to make contact, not enough to aggravate the tension and pain that were harbored there.

"What are you doing?" he finally asked, the words coming out of his mouth in slow motion. When he received no answer, his eyes shifted to Shawn who seemed content just to sit and wait. "What is she doing?"

"Making you better," Shana's father answered matter-of-factly. "Don't fight it, boy, the girl's got magic hands. You should see what she can do to a man's spine. Make him feel like a kid again. 'Course, in your case, that's not much of a trip, but for someone like me…" He chuckled. "Well, it covers a lot more territory than I like to think about. But she can make you feel brand new." There was unabashed affection in the man's eyes as he looked at Shana. "Don't know where I would be without her."

"You'd be fine, Dad," she assured him. Travis could hear the smile in her voice.

"Not by a long shot." The tone of his voice changed as he added. "Susan would have never looked after me the way you do."

"Susan?" Travis asked, looking at Shawn. "Is that another daughter? Or your wife?"

"My wife passed two years ago," Shawn informed him stiffly. Travis had a feeling the shift in tone was to keep the emotion from gaining control of him. But he could see the pain in the man's eyes. Two years and he still missed her. It was nice to know that love actually did enter some people's lives for more than a weekend. "Susan's my daughter."

"How many do you have?" Travis asked, desperately struggling to focus on the conversation and not the woman whose fingertips still moved seductively along his temples.

"There's just Susan and Shana," Shawn said, "now that Grace's gone."

"Grace?"

"My wife," Shawn clarified. He nodded toward Shana behind him. "How's that feel?"

"Good," Travis admitted.

But he knew nothing could be done for the pain he was experiencing. The headache had to run its course. He still fed it aspirins because a part of him was ever hopeful that, this one time, he could beat it back with pills. It was mostly a useless endeavor.

"But I don't want to waste your time," he added, intending the remark for Shana. He tried to turn his head, but paid dearly for that. The resulting pain shot through the top of his head, his nose and his jaw.

To his surprise, Shana didn't withdraw her hands but continued massaging, making her small circles against his temples, sliding her fingertips in progressively larger and larger areas.

"Shh," she soothed. "You have to give it a little time," she advised. "The pain will go away soon, I promise."

Not soon enough for him, he thought sarcastically. Hopefully before he liquefied right in front of her. It became increasingly more difficult to concentrate on what the woman's father was saying when she stood behind him like that, wrecking havoc on his temples as well as his system. Her perfume, something light, heady and seductive as hell, seemed to seep into all his senses.

Ordinarily, in his present condition, the scent—any scent—would just contribute to his headache. But for some reason, hers didn't. Instead, it soothed him even as it aroused him.

How was that possible?

"Dad, you and Mr. Marlowe go on talking," Shana was saying. She'd bent forward ever so slightly as she spoke, just enough for him to feel her leaning lightly against his back.

Every nerve ending in his body felt as if it as hot-wired.

"You familiar with my restaurant?" Shawn was asking him.

With effort, Travis focused. "I don't know," he admitted. "What's it called?"

Right now, if the man called the restaurant after himself, Travis wouldn't have been able to make the connection. His brain was taking a definite time-out. He was struggling not just with an all-invasive headache, but with a sudden, startling desire to pull Shana onto his lap. Not just to pull her onto his lap, but to kiss her, as well.

Definitely not his style.

Not that he aspired to the role of hermit or someone who lived and breathed work to the point that he did nothing else, but he had become the controlled one in his family. The one who always thought things out, looked at the consequences of any action. He was no longer given to the rash behavior of his childhood.

So what were these urges doing, suddenly dancing through him with reckless abandon?

"Shawn's Li'l Bit of Heaven." Travis realized that he had been staring at the man, because Shawn added, "That's the name of the restaurant. I named it for my daughter," he confided.

"Shana?" Because if that was the case, Travis couldn't help thinking, the man was given to serious understatement.

Shawn flushed and his complexion instantly turned a ruddy shade. "No," he corrected, "Susan. That's...my older girl," he said after a moment's hesitation. And then, because the woman's presence was conspicuously absent, he added, "She couldn't come. She's been too busy to take time out for her old man these days," Shawn grumbled. The frown on his face seemed to go deep, down to the very bone.

And then, the next moment, the man's frown vanished and he was jovial again, caught up in a memory.

"But you should've seen her as a little bit of a thing. Sunshine in a bottle, that was her. Or maybe I should've said sunshine *with* a bottle," he chuckled at his own joke. "She was a baby back then. Once she started walking and talking, she made it clear right from the beginning that she marched to her own tune." He cleared his throat, pushing away whatever thought was troubling him. He raised his eyes to Travis's face. "Anyway, you hear of it?"

Saying yes might leave him open to questions that he couldn't answer. At the risk of bruising the man's ego, Travis said, "I'm afraid not."

To his surprise, rather than look put out, Shawn smiled and nodded. "The truth. You could've lied, trying to get on my good side, but you didn't. You told the truth. I like that." He nodded his head several more times, as if carrying on a debate that only he could hear. And then his eyes lit up. "Okay, boy, I'm gonna go with you." He eyed him closely. "I'm putting my trust in you. Don't let me down."

"Thank you," Travis said with feeling. "I won't let you down." Still seated, he slid forward and extended his hand to the man. At the same time, he felt Shana withdraw her fingertips from his temples.

For a moment, he thought it was because he was leaning forward.

And then it hit him.

Raising his eyes to her face as she came around to rejoin her father on the sofa, Travis stared at her incredulously.

"It's gone," he said like a mesmerized child watching a magician who had just made a full-grown tiger disappear from the stage. "My headache's gone." He was stunned. Migraine headaches, when they came, which fortunately for him was not often, moved in for the duration of the day. Sometimes longer. "That's not possible," he murmured.

Shana smiled at him. "Is your head throbbing?" she asked innocently.

"No."

The look of pure satisfaction that came to her face was spellbinding to watch. "Then it's possible," she concluded.

Shawn chuckled, clearly pleased with the outcome. "Didn't I tell you she was something?"

She certainly was. And the fact that her fingertips seemed to work miracles had nothing to do with it.

Chapter 3

The first meeting ended with Travis giving Shawn O'Reilly a list of documents he needed to review in order to ultimately place them beneath the protective umbrella of a living trust. In exchange, Shawn tendered an invitation to Travis to drop by the restaurant for a "meal that you'll never forget."

Whether by instinct or because being in such close proximity to Shana had temporarily rendered his ordinarily sharp thought process null and void, Travis refrained from mentioning that one of his brothers was a chef and owner of the popular Kate's Kitchen, a five-star restaurant overlooking the ocean in Laguna Beach. Trevor had named the restaurant as a tribute to their stepmother because of all the encouragement she'd given him over the years.

Travis accepted the light-green business card that Shawn held out to him, tucking it into his wallet.

"What about our next appointment?" Shawn asked.

Travis flipped through several pages on his desk calendar, searching for an empty block of time. "How's two weeks from tomorrow at ten sound?" he asked. Fully expecting the man to agree to the date, Travis picked up his pen and was about to write in Shawn's name when the man stopped him.

"Don't you have anything sooner?" Shawn prodded. "I'd like it sooner than later," he added, then explained, "I'm really not a very patient man and when I make up my mind, I like to see things start moving. You understand how it is."

It was a perfectly plausible explanation, one Travis felt confident was used by countless people every day. Impatience was a by-product of the present fast-forward, fast-track world. Yet for some unknown reason, Travis couldn't quite shake the feeling that Shawn was leaving something unsaid. That the man's motivation for the request and his desire for speed was driven by something other than just impatience.

Travis didn't push the subject.

But it did make him curious.

Travis worked his way backward through the calendar, starting with the slot two weeks in the future. Every space seemed to be taken. Business was good, he thought, but by the same token, it did make things difficult if he wanted to get O'Reilly in earlier.

He decided to give up his lunch. "How about two days from today, at noon?" he suggested. "Does that work better for you?"

"Don't you ordinarily eat lunch around then?" Shana asked.

Travis dismissed the question. "I can send out for a sandwich later on," he told her. "No problem."

"Or, I can bring you something from the restaurant," Shawn offered. "We'll be here," he said, confirming the appointment. "And in the meantime," the man went on, "you come on by the restaurant tonight. Say, around eight? Unless you've got other plans." His expression, though amiable, challenged him to come up with an acceptable excuse for not showing up at his restaurant this evening.

Travis did have other plans. Communing with his pillow and catching up on some well-earned sleep before he drifted into the land of the zombies. But he couldn't very well turn down the enthusiastic invitation. For whatever reason, having him drop by to see the restaurant seemed to mean too much to his new client.

He wondered if Shana would be there.

"No," Travis answered, "no other plans."

Shawn immediately beamed in response even though, from his behavior, the outcome was a foregone conclusion to the man.

"Good, then we'll see you there." He nodded.

Hope bubbled up inside of him. Travis shifted his glance to include Shana before asking, "We?"

"Shana's my right hand," O'Reilly told him with a great deal of pride. "In more ways than one." He groaned at the end of the second sentence as he attempted to get up from the sofa. Instantly, Shana tucked her arm through his, providing the leverage and support he needed to rise. "Couldn't run that without her, either." He took a deep breath, like someone who had just made it to the top of a mountain and then shook his head sadly. "Don't get old if you can help it, boy. There's little dignity to it."

"Don't talk nonsense, Dad. You've got enough dignity for two people. You're just a little creaky right now, that's all," Shana comforted simply.

Her arm still threaded through her father's, she gently guided Shawn to the door. Opening it, he stepped across the threshold and was out in the hall when Shana suddenly remembered that she'd left her purse on the sofa.

Reentering the room, she flashed a conspiratorial smile at Travis who was about to follow them out. She'd left her purse behind on purpose, wanting the opportunity to get the attorney alone for a moment.

"You don't have to come if you have other plans," she told him, lowering her voice. "Dad tends to overwhelm people a bit. It's the Texas in him," she added with a laugh.

Her laugh was like music, Travis thought. Spellbinding music. It took him more than a second to shake himself free.

"That's all right," he assured her. "I really don't have any plans." And even if he had, he wouldn't have passed up this opportunity, not if she was going to be there.

"No more midnight-oil burning?" Shana asked innocently.

Her eyes were smiling. He liked that. They seemed to highlight her entire face—making it even more perfect.

"I try not to do that two nights in a row," he told her as he reached for the still-cold coffee on his desk. "It makes me a little sluggish mentally in the morning."

"Don't worry, I'll make sure you get to bed early," she promised.

He'd just raised the coffee cup to his lips and taken a sip. Hearing her comment caused the coffee to slide down the wrong way. He started coughing.

Instantly alert, Shana quickly crossed over to him and began to pound him on the back. Still coughing, Travis held up his hand, signaling that he was all right.

"Excuse me?" he finally got out, albeit rather hoarsely.

Shana replayed her last words, then grinned. If she realized how he'd interpreted the line, she gave no further indication.

"Dad has a tendency to do a lot of buttonholing at the restaurant. Sometimes he doesn't know when to stop. He's got a thousand stories to tell," she explained. "I'll just make sure you go home at a decent hour so you get some sleep."

"Oh."

The single word echoed simultaneously with enlightenment and just a touch of disappointment. For a moment there, he'd let his mind drift and her words conjured up an image he'd found both infinitely pleasing and damn arousing.

Of course that was what she meant. He knew that. What was the matter with him? "That's all right," he told her. "I come from a large family. I know how to make an exit without hurting anyone's feelings."

"Then I'll look forward to seeing you tonight," Shana said. "We're right in the middle of the block. You can't miss us." Humor curved her lips and then she winked. "We're the ones with a shamrock in the sign."

With that, she left the room and joined her father. Travis heard them walking away, their voices growing fainter as they made their way down the hall to the elevator.

Shana's wink had repercussions. Travis felt as if he'd just been shot with another arrow. Unlike the ones that had assaulted his temple earlier, this one had a soft tip and went straight to his heart.

He slid bonelessly back into his chair.

To the best of Travis's recollection, he'd never responded to a woman like this before. Oh, there'd been attractive, even beautiful women who had crossed his path, but he couldn't recall a single one making him feel as if he'd been struck by lightning. And been happy about it.

Shifting to slip his hand into his pocket, he pulled out his wallet and took out the card Shawn had handed him. He stared at it, committing the address to memory just in case he lost the card between now and this evening. It was a date he intended to keep. For a number of reasons. And humoring a client was way down on the list.

"You're checking out another restaurant?" Even over the phone, Trevor's voice sounded incredulous when Travis called him later that afternoon.

"Not checking it out, I'm seeing a client there," Travis explained.

So far, Travis hadn't been able to get to the crux of why he'd called. Trevor sounded a bit harried and definitely put out that he was asking about another restaurant.

"Why don't you bring him over to mine?" Trevor suggested. "I'll make your personal favorite," he coaxed, adding, "on the house. You can pretend to pick up the check to impress your client and I'll reimburse you the next time I see you. See, the best of all worlds. Besides, you've been so busy, I haven't had a chance to see you lately."

"Look in the mirror," Travis quipped. "That's almost like seeing me."

"We're not mirror images of each other," Trevor reminded him. There was a noise in the background and for a moment, Travis heard the sound of a hand being placed over the receiver. Trevor's muffled voice called to his assistant, Emilio, to take care of a late delivery. When his attention returned to his telephone conversation with Travis, he said, "You, Trent and I are identical images of each other." And then a thought obviously struck Trevor. "Unless you don't want him to see me because it might confuse him. It is a *him* that we're talking about, aren't we?"

"It's a him." Travis thought it prudent not to mention Shana or the odd, almost overwhelming attraction he felt for her. Ever since his brothers had married, they waited for him to make the set complete. Telling Trevor about Shana would just set his brother off on a tangent that really had no basis in reality. "The restaurant I just asked you about belongs to my client," Travis explained. "He wants me to drop by to see it."

"Why?"

"Because I get the feeling that he's as proud of it as you are of yours."

There was a slight pause and Trevor capitulated. "What did you say the name of it was again?"

That was more like it. This was the reason why he'd called Trevor in the first place. He'd assumed that, just like lawyers and doctors, restaurant owners had their own little network, keeping tabs on one another and being more in the know about a particular restaurant than the average person on the street.

"Shawn's Li'l Bit of Heaven," Travis told him. "Have you heard of it?"

"Rings a bell," Trevor admitted. The silence told Travis his brother was trying to remember something. "They specialize in Irish food—and in Tex-Mex. To each his own, but it's a strange combination if you ask me."

"Not if you know the owner," Travis told him. "The man's from Texas and he had ties to Ireland somewhere along the line in his ancestry. His last name's O'Reilly."

"Ah. And another mystery has been laid to rest," Trevor cracked. "I can ask around if you want," he offered. "Just what is it you want to know?"

"If the restaurant is doing well. If there were any health code violations in the last year, things like that. The usual. I need to assess its present value," he explained.

"Is the owner selling it?" Trevor asked, mildly interested. He'd been toying with the idea of opening a second restaurant and leaving Emilio to run the one presently open.

"No, he wants to put it into a living trust for his daughters."

There was a low whistle on the other end of the line. "Nice," Trevor commented. "But instead of taking the roundabout route, why don't you just ask to look at his books?"

"I will, but I thought I'd get a heads up first so that I'd know what to expect," Travis confided. "O'Reilly invited me to drop by for a meal tonight. It's strictly social."

"All right, I'll see what I can find out," Trevor said. "I can have Venus ask around. If anyone has 'dirt' on anything, those high-society people she used to hang out with would probably be the first to know."

The mention of Trevor's wife momentarily took the conversation in another direction. "So she still wants us to call her Venus, huh?"

The idea amused him. "Venus" was the name his brother had given her the night he'd rescued the woman who eventually became his wife from a watery grave. When Trevor had finally managed to pull her to shore, she had absolutely no recollection of who she was or how she happened to land in the middle of the water.

It was only after Trevor had built a relationship with the woman and fallen hopelessly in love with her that Venus's memory returned. Rather than someone who had fallen on hard times and was down on her luck, she turned out to be the heiress of a vast fortune. She had accidentally fallen overboard while attempting to escape from a yacht and a pending wedding ceremony that would have bound her to a man she ultimately decided she didn't love.

"As far as I'm concerned," Trevor told him with feeling, "she *is* Venus."

Travis laughed softly to himself. "Works for me," he said.

"No offense, brother," Trevor responded genially, "but that really doesn't have top priority in the equation."

He saw the light on his phone turn on. Bea's way of letting him know his next appointment was here. It was time to go. "Just see what you can find out for me, okay?"

"When do you need to know?"

Travis glanced at the desk calendar to see who his next appointment was. On days like today, people tended to run together. And if not for Shana, he recalled with no small amount of gratitude, he'd really be in a bad way because he'd still have his migraine. "As soon as you can would be nice."

He heard his brother laugh. "That's what I love about you, Trav. You're never in a hurry."

Trevor should talk, he thought. But he chose neutral ground for his response. "Hey, compared to Kelsey, I'm standing still."

"Compared to Kelsey, a hurricane is standing still," Trevor said with a laugh. "I'll get back to you," he promised.

"You do that," Travis said, ending the conversation.

Hanging up, he slipped Shawn's business card back into his wallet. It was already getting worn around the edges.

For no reason, an image of Shana flashed across his mind's eye.

It had to be lack of sleep that made him act like this, he decided. Like some adolescent with a terminal case of overactive hormones. Hell, he thought, even when he'd been a teenager, he hadn't behaved so intensely.

Although there was that time when he and Trent had switched places, going out with each other's girl-friends just to see if the girls could tell them apart. Problem was, he'd found himself falling for Trent's girl. There'd been a lot of guilt involved before he finally confessed his feelings to Trent. When he did, to his relief, Trent told him that he really wasn't that into the girl.

Trent's heart really belonged to Laurel Valentine, the girl who, years later, became his wife.

The romance between Travis and Trent's former girl hadn't fared nearly that well. It lasted all of three months. Like a flash fire, it was way too hot not to burn out.

But even that hadn't felt like this, Travis thought.

Of course, back then, he was getting enough sleep, he recalled with a touch of humor.

Glancing at his calendar again, he saw that, merci-fully, he only had two more appointments for the day. And, for once, there were no court appearances sche-duled in the late afternoon, like yesterday.

He was going home right after the last appointment, he told himself. What he needed before he went to the restaurant was a well-deserved nap. Lucky for him, he could fall asleep pretty quickly.

That was what he needed. Just some sleep and then, although beautiful, Shana O'Reilly would no longer look like an earthbound angel to him.

He leaned forward and pressed the intercom on his desk. "Please send Mrs. Baxter in, Bea."

He thought he heard her murmur "It's about time," but he couldn't be sure and there was no way he would ask her to repeat herself.

Kate hadn't raised any stupid children, he thought with a smile as he rose to greet his next client.

Chapter 4

Twilight lightly embraced the parking lot as Travis got out of his vehicle and crossed to the front door of Shawn's Li'l Bit of Heaven.

He wasn't sure just what to expect.

A great many restaurants elected to go with a motif, a decor that identified them and defined the way they saw themselves. Walking through Shawn's heavy oak double doors was like stepping into a sprawled-out country kitchen.

Unlike the cuisine it favored, the restaurant's decor was neither Irish nor Mexican. Instead, it seemed dedicated to the concept of the perennial family gathering place of old: the kitchen where discussions were held, homework was done and food was prepared and enjoyed.

Rather than the slightly darkened atmosphere that other eating establishments favored, Shawn's was brightly lit so that people could not only see one another at the table, but were able to make out the faces of the patrons at neighboring tables.

One big, happy dining experience, Travis thought. He looked around the general area, trying to spot either Shawn or his daughter. The restaurant was fairly full, not a bad accomplishment for a Tuesday when most people took their evening meal at home instead of going out.

"You made it."

The words were uttered behind him. He didn't have to turn around to know that the melodic voice belonged to Shana. But he turned around anyway, a tiny part of him hoping that she wouldn't appear quite as beautiful at their second meeting as she had at their first.

If anything, she was even more beautiful.

Her long blond hair worn loose about her shoulders, Shana wore a peasant blouse and a wide, colorful skirt that easily fit into either one of the two cultures associated with the restaurant. Strategically placed on the white blouse was a small pin that identified her in ornate letters as "Shana." Beneath her name was the title "hostess."

"You work here?" Travis heard himself asking in surprise. He hadn't pictured her showing people to their tables. Did princesses have a day job?

Amused by his question, she inclined her head slightly. "I help out when I can. Besides, Dad's here every night, so it gives me something to do instead of sitting around just watching him."

He wasn't sure that he followed her meaning. "Watching him?"

The smile on her lips seemed to grow a shade tighter. "My father doesn't like to admit it, but he needs help getting around. So I help," she said simply. "Do you have a preference?"

He stared at her. "Excuse me?"

She gestured toward the dining area. "Your table," she explained. "Do you have a preference where you want to sit? Some people like to be as far away from the kitchen as possible. Others want to be in the center of the room so they can see everything."

As long as he could see her, it didn't matter. "Anywhere is fine."

"A man who's easily pleased. I like that." Sending a warm smile his way, she picked up a menu from the hostess desk and led the way into the dining area.

Music blended in with the voices of the various patrons, weaving a tapestry of noise that was oddly soothing.

Travis was doing his best to focus exclusively on his role as an impartial family lawyer but it definitely was not as easy as he would have liked. When she spoke, Shana became animated, gesturing to underscore her words. And each gesture caused the neckline of her peasant blouse to dip and move, rendering enticing glimpses of soft, perfect cleavage, the sight of which effectively kidnapped him away from thoughts of all things lawyerly.

"This table all right?" she asked, selecting one that was slightly right of center.

"It's fine," he told her, his eyes on her, not the table in question. If she'd offered it, he would have agreed to sit on a toadstool.

Get a grip, Trav, or she's going to think her father's employing a babbling idiot.

Taking a seat, he accepted the menu from her. Ambition had always been a driving force in his life. It generated the next question he put to her. "How old are you if you don't mind my asking?"

She studied him for a long moment before speaking. "That depends."

He felt his breath catching in his throat and he forced it out. "On?"

"Are you asking the question as our lawyer, or as my father's guest?"

He tried to gauge which was the better answer and which would get him a response, because he had a feeling that they weren't equal in her eyes. He went with what was safe. "As your lawyer."

"Then I'm twenty-five," she told him.

The first thing that registered was that she was two years younger than he was. He forced himself back on track.

"I'm assuming you have a degree." She seemed far too intelligent to have just floated aimlessly after high school, living off her father.

"I do." Amusement entered her eyes as she second-guessed what he was getting at. "You think I should be some fledgling barracuda sailing down the fast lane in pursuit of a mega career."

That was a little blunter than he would have worded it, but she'd gotten the gist of it. "Not exactly in those terms, but I'd think you would be more motivated than this. Don't you want to forge a career for yourself?"

She seemed to take no offense from his suggestion. "I have a career, Mr. Marlowe. I'm the hostess here. It allows me to meet a variety of interesting people I might not meet at another job. *And,* more importantly, I am also my father's caregiver. With me around, he doesn't quite feel the sting of his infirmities as strongly as he might if someone else was hovering over him, offering to help when his strength fails him."

Caregiver.

He understood feelings like that. They fit right in with the way things were done in his own family. It was also nice to discover other people valued home and family the way he did.

He found himself being more and more attracted to Shana. It was a definite conflict of interest, he warned himself.

"He means a lot to you, doesn't he?" Travis asked warmly.

"He means the world to me," she corrected and then added, "He's my dad. I'd walk through fire for him—and he'd do the same for me," she told him with feeling. "We've gotten even closer since my mother died," she confided. "I couldn't leave him to deal with things on his own, even if I wanted to—and I don't," she underscored in case Travis had another comment to offer about her choice of vocations.

If she had a career the way he seemed to think she should, she wouldn't have been able to devote as much time to her father as she did. And she wanted to spend time with him. There was this vague feeling buzzing around inside her that time was short.

"I noticed he had trouble getting up from the sofa this morning," Travis acknowledged. He lowered his voice, as if this was something he understood was private and she didn't have to answer him if she didn't want to. "What's wrong with him, if you don't mind my asking."

"If I did, you'd probably only go to the source." Travis didn't strike her as a man who backed off until he had what he was after. "My father has a number of things going wrong at the same time." She deliberately divorced herself from her words. If she didn't, she knew she would tear up and although he seemed very amiable, Travis was still a stranger. "He has emphysema, a result of a cigarette habit he started at the age of eleven and didn't stop until he turned sixty-five. Plus there's angina—he's on heart medication," she told Travis before he had the opportunity to ask. "There are also a few other minor conditions, all of which keep him from being the dynamic man he used to be."

Travis thought of the first impression Shawn made on him this morning. "Oh, I don't know, he seemed pretty dynamic to me."

Shana smiled fondly. "You should have seen him when I was a little girl. He seemed to be able to go for days without stopping." She'd worshipped the ground her father had walked on. "I'd come home from school, rush through my homework and then sit by the window, waiting for him to come home. When he did—and I was still awake," she added with a laugh because there were many nights when she'd fall asleep waiting, "he'd always pick me up, swing me around and ride me around on his shoulders.

"They seemed like the broadest shoulders in the world to me then." She let a sigh escape, then flushed ruefully, as if that qualification somehow made her disloyal to her father. "Back then I thought he would go on forever. That he was immortal." Her voice took on a tinge of sadness. "I think he thought so, too."

"It's a common feeling," Travis told her. He had so many clients who had been coerced by their families to get their affairs in order and prepare a will. "Until someone close to you dies."

She looked at him sharply, catching something in his voice. "Who died who was close to you?"

He wasn't here to talk about himself. Backing off, he said, "I was just speaking in general."

Shana looked into his eyes and then slowly shook her head.

"No, you weren't," she countered quietly.

He had no idea how she knew. Maybe those luminescent blue eyes of hers allowed her to look into his soul, maybe not. Either way, he saw no reason to pretend that she was wrong. He didn't believe in lying.

"My mother."

His answer surprised her. "You lost your mother, too?"

It gave them something in common. Without realizing it, she felt a little closer to him. "When?"

Why was it always painful, going back to that time? He was twenty-two years past it. The memory should have healed by now.

"I was five at the time."

She looked at him with sympathy. She'd felt devastated when she lost her mother two years ago. How much worse was that kind of a loss for a little boy? For a moment, she took a seat at the table, placing her hand on his in silent empathy.

"That must have been terrible for you."

"It was," he agreed. He'd made a vow never to dwell on that time, but to acknowledge it and move on. Because, for all intents and purposes, his life had done the same. "But luckily, after several very huge misses, my father struck gold when he finally hired Kate to be our nanny."

Shana heard the wealth of affection in his voice. Whoever this woman was, she meant a great deal to him.

"Kate?"

"She's my stepmother. She has been for over twenty years. Even in the early days, before she married my father, Kate made a world of difference to all of us, thank God. I think my brothers and I were destined for juvenile hall if she hadn't come into our lives and straightened us out."

"So she was a disciplinarian?" Shana guessed. She tried to picture the man in front of her being a difficult child and couldn't do it.

"Just the opposite. At the time, she was a child-psychology student with an abundant amount of patience and love." And then, as if hearing what he was saying for the first time, Travis stopped talking and looked at her in surprise. "How did we get on this subject? I'm supposed to be the one asking the questions."

The smile Shana gave him told him she was very good at turning the tables on people, usually without them knowing it.

"A little mutual sharing never hurt," she told him. "Besides, it makes you a little more human and accessible to us."

He never thought of himself in any other way. Kate had set a very good example. "I'm always accessible to my clients."

Her mouth curved, more intrigued by what he wasn't saying. "But are you human?"

"That's decided on a case-by-case basis."

Any further exchange between them was cut short. Shawn O'Reilly, smartly dressed in a navy blue jacket, light gray slacks and a very light blue shirt, joined them. His very presence overwhelmed any sense of intimacy that might have been fostered.

Clapping Travis lightly on the back, he happily declared the same thing that Shana had when she first saw him. "You came." Digging his knuckles into the table for support, he lowered himself into the chair opposite Travis. The chair that Shana had just vacated.

"I already used that line, Dad," Shana teased, unwrapping his utensils from within a deep-green woven napkin. Without looking, she placed the cutlery on either side of his hands.

"Speaking of lines," Shawn nodded toward the room's entrance, "it looks like there's one forming at the hostess desk."

Shana quickly glanced over her shoulder. Two separate parties had gathered there. Several of the people were looking around for someone to come and seat them.

"Whoops." She flashed a quick grin at Travis. "I guess talking to Mr. Marlowe here made me forget I'm still on duty. I'll leave him in your hands, Dad. I'm sure you can entertain him with your stories." Raising her hand, Shana signaled to catch the attention of a nearby waitress. Making eye contact, the young woman nodded. "Becka will take your orders and bring you both something to eat."

"She fusses too much over me," Shawn confided as he watched Shana hurry back to the hostess desk. His bright blue eyes shifted back to Travis. "I have to admit I like it, though. It's nice to know that someone cares about you."

Travis had gotten very good at hearing things that weren't being said. It helped when delving into a client's history, allowing him to coax things into the light of day that might otherwise remain hidden.

"You and your other daughter aren't close, I take it?"

For a moment, the older man looked just a shade confused. And then he seemed to understand what was being asked.

"Oh, you mean Susan? No, we're not. Not because

I wouldn't like it," he added quickly and with a touch of sadness. "That's Susan's choice." He sighed, shaking his head. "Susan has always followed some path that never made any sense to me. And stubborn? She loved flaunting her independence at me. If I said 'don't play in traffic,' she'd grab her ball and head straight for the intersection. She always seemed to get a big kick out of going against everything I said to her." Reaching for a small loaf of bread, he began to slice it on the miniature cutting board provided. "Turned my hair gray long before its time." Finished with one slice, he slipped it onto Travis's bread plate, then turned his attention to slicing a second one for himself.

Travis nodded his thanks. The bread still felt warm when he picked it up. "What about Shana?"

The sadness instantly vanished from Shawn's face. "Shana turned out to be my saving grace. Definite comfort in my old age."

Because he felt he should, Travis took a bite of the bread. "Tasty," he commented. "But no, what I meant was, how does Shana get along with her sister?"

A hint of resigned disappointment entered Shawn's voice. "She doesn't." Realizing how that might sound, he was quick to absolve Shana of any blame. "Oh, Shana would put up with her if Susan was here, even though when she was, Susan always bossed her around. That's just the kind of girl Shana is. She doesn't hold a grudge. But Susan's a whole different story. She always wanted to be free, no ties. No time for anyone in the family. She always acted as if the sun rose and set around her. Never a thought for anyone else. Damn near killed her mother when she—"

Shawn stopped abruptly, as if realizing where he was heading with his words—to a place that couldn't be exposed yet.

He coughed and switched directions.

"She'd occasionally spend the night at the house, but that was only when she and her current boyfriend-of-the-month were on the outs. She has a key," he explained. "She'd come in late and crash in her old room, sleep until noon and then get up and bum around the house as if she'd never left. Her mother would try to talk her into moving back in, but it never lasted long. Susan'd make up with her boyfriend or she'd find some other lowlife to take his place and she'd be gone again, no word to anyone."

It definitely sounded as if they were better off without her. Travis kept the thought to himself. "How old is she?"

Shawn paused, searching his memory in the way of fathers who had always left things like age and birthdays to their spouse to remember.

"Forty-two," he finally said triumphantly, pleased with himself for actually remembering. "Last December seventeenth," he added for good measure.

"And no other children?" He needed to know that for the will. And, he had to admit, to satisfy his own curiosity about the family dynamics.

Shawn sounded genuine remorseful as he shook his head and said, "No."

Travis did a quick calculation. There was seventeen

years between the sisters. "Spaced them pretty far apart, didn't you?"

"Shana was a surprise," Shawn said honestly. "She definitely wasn't planned the way Susan was." The laugh was self-deprecating as well as rueful. "Sometimes it's the unplanned things that turn out the best." He laughed again. The laugh transformed into a cough. The latter quickly became overwhelming. After a minute, it looked as if he wasn't going to be able to stop.

The waitress, Becka, hurried over to their table, a shy, apologetic expression on her face.

"Sorry," she announced, "but table three wanted to change their order after the meals came out." Her brown eyes widened as she look at her employer. "Do you want me to get you a glass of water Mr. O'Reilly?"

Shawn was coughing too hard to answer.

Travis began to get concerned. He wondered if he should ask the waitress to bring Shana over, then decided that maybe he should give the water a try first.

"I think that would be an excellent idea," Travis told her.

But Shawn waved his hand dismissively above his head as he struggled to contain his cough. Feeling impotent, Travis watched him a moment longer. And then, to his relief, Shawn's cough began to subside.

Shawn dragged in a huge gulp of air. "Sorry about that," he said to Travis, exhaling rather shakily. Turning to waitress, he gave his order, then stopped to reassure her. "It's okay, Becka. Something just went down the wrong way. Bring me the usual," he told her.

She bobbed her head, not bothering to write down the order. Becka turned her brown eyes toward Travis.

"And you, sir?"

Everything on the menu looked delicious. He raised his eyes to Shawn. "Is the 'usual' good?"

Shawn nodded with feeling. Pride entered his reddened face. "Damn sure is. I've got only the best people working for me in the kitchen."

Travis closed the menu and placed it on top of the one Shawn hadn't opened. "Make that two 'usuals,'" he told the waitress.

Shawn smiled in appreciation as Becka hurried to the kitchen. "That's what I like," he told Travis. "A man who's willing to take a chance, sight unseen."

In light of the gleam that had entered Shawn's eyes, Travis couldn't help wondering if he'd just made a rash mistake that his taste buds would regret.

Chapter 5

The "usual" turned out to be the unlikely combination platter of a three-cheese quesadilla with a side order of corned beef.

"Never liked cabbage," Shawn confided to him as he dug into his dinner. As he spoke, the man still watched him intently, as if to get his honest reaction to the meal. "Although I have to say that the guy I've got running the kitchen makes one hell of a serving of cabbage if you like that sort of thing—bits of fried onion and crumbled bacon pieces mixed in with deep-fried cabbage." His knife and fork, in constant motion, were stilled for a moment as he offered, "I could have them bring you some if you like."

Where was the man putting all this? Travis couldn't

help wondering. He was eating like a man recently rescued from a deserted island. His own stomach was already pretty full.

"No, this is quite enough," Travis assured his host. The serving was large. "I'll probably need a doggie bag as it is." He leaned back, surveying what was still left. "This has to be the largest portion I've ever seen."

"We do everything large in Texas," Shawn boasted, tickled. "Even when we're not in Texas at the time. So?" he prodded eagerly, nodding at the plate in front of him. "What do you think?"

Travis was reminded of the way Trevor looked while waiting to hear if a new recipe was a success. Luckily, he could be honest with the man. "This is probably the best quesadilla and the best corned beef I've ever had."

Shawn grinned like a child who'd just been awarded a long anticipated gold star. "Knew you'd like it." And then he glanced toward the front of the restaurant before leaning in closer. "Do me a favor, though."

The lawyer in him tended to be cautious about making promises, especially ones whose parameters hadn't been spelled out yet. But the child in him that Kate had raised tended to be far more open and trusting in every way. Travis found that he was at odds with himself. But he couldn't see any harm in accommodating this man who ate with such gusto.

"Sure," he said gamely. "What is it?"

Shawn lowered his voice slightly, as if he was leery of being overheard.

"Don't tell Shana I had this, all right?" He continued

eating as he spoke, like a man who anticipated being separated from his food. "If she had her way, she'd have me eating nothing but vegetables and swallowing vitamins all day long."

Travis couldn't help smiling. "She's just looking out for you."

Shawn sighed, reluctantly nodding his head. "I know, but it's the quality of life as well as the quantity, you know? If I follow her diet, I won't really live longer, it'll just feel that way."

While understanding Shana's intent, Travis still sympathized with the man. He glanced over to the hostess desk. Shana's back was to them.

"If you want to keep this a secret from her, don't you think you should be eating somewhere else?"

"You have a point," Shawn acknowledged as he continued savoring his meal. "Lucky for me, she'll forgive me after the lecture."

"Lecture?"

Shawn chuckled. It was obvious that he loved his daughter very much.

"She always gives me a lecture, makes me feel guilty because indulging like this might take me away from her sooner than she'd like." And then he grew serious. "But nobody lives forever, right?"

"No, they don't," Travis agreed. He carefully took the middle ground. "But by the same token, they don't necessarily need to play Russian roulette with things that are bad for them."

The serious moment over, Shawn slipped another

forkful of corned beef between his lips and smiled in contentment. "How can anything this good be bad for you?" he wondered out loud. "Melts on your tongue, boy. Just melts on your tongue."

At that moment, Shana, leading a party of six to one of the larger tables in the dining room, passed by their table. Her eyes were instantly drawn to what was on Shawn's plate. Travis saw Shawn bracing himself. But if his daughter disapproved, she gave no indication.

"I guess she didn't notice," Travis said after Shana was out of earshot.

"Oh, she noticed all right," Shawn assured him. He began eating faster, anticipating what was to come. "Eyes like a hawk, that one. Takes in everything."

Travis smiled to himself. The description reminded him of the way they'd all felt about Kate when she'd first come to live with them. For a long time, he and his brothers were convinced that she had eyes in the back of her head as well because absolutely *nothing* ever got by her.

Shawn didn't have long to wait to be proven right. Two minutes later, after seating the people she'd been leading, Shana returned to their table. Her hands were on her hips and there was a reproving look on her face.

"What did I tell you about eating all that fat?" she asked Shawn.

Shawn turned almost sheepish. "Not in front of a guest, Shana."

Shana refused to back down. "Oh no, Old Man, that doesn't fly." She gestured toward Travis. "He's not a guest, he's our lawyer, Dad. Our *family* lawyer," she empha-

sized. "That means that he gets to know us, warts and all."
Leaning over, she took the dinner plate away from him.

"Aw, Shana," he protested, but he made no effort to
lay claim to the plate.

"I'll have Becka bring you the sautéed vegetable
platter." Looking at the plate in her hand, she relented
only marginally. "I'll tell her to have the chef sprinkle
bacon-flavored bits on it."

"Bacon-*flavored* bits," Shawn repeated dismissively.
"That's just not the same thing." He sighed dramatically
for effect.

"It'll have to do," she told him, refusing to give in
despite the fact that he was tugging on her heart strings.
"You've had enough fat for one day."

And then, at the same moment, both Shana and
Shawn turned to Travis and said the same exact thing.
"See what I have to put up with?" Any potential tension
was immediately erased.

Travis laughed. "She's trying to keep you around a
little longer," he told Shawn. "There's nothing wrong
with that."

Shana smiled warmly at him. "Nice to have an ally."
She looked over toward the waitress who had brought
Shawn the dinner she'd just confiscated. "I've told
everyone here not to give him anything fatty to eat but
they're afraid to say no to the 'boss.'"

"And well they should be," Shawn replied, pleased.
"If they value their jobs."

Shana laughed shortly. "You couldn't fire anyone
and you know it," she told her father. Her eyes shifted

toward Travis. "He's a big pushover, no matter how much he huffs and puffs."

"A little respect for your elders." Shawn tried to look stern as he issued the warning.

He got no argument from her on that point. "Fine. When you start acting like an 'elder,' I'll give you all the respect you want." She paused to lean over and brush a quick kiss on his cheek. "Now, be a good boy, Dad, and have the vegetable platter when I send it out."

Shawn sniffed, rejecting her instruction. "Not hungry anymore."

She took another look at the plate she was holding, then sighed. Her father had done justice to it. Despite the oversize portion he'd been served, Shawn had consumed more than half of the meal in the time that it took Travis to eat less than a quarter of his.

"Small wonder," she observed. "All right, no vegetables. I'll just send Becka over with tea," she told Shawn. "Decaf," she added before her father could say anything.

Handing the plate to the busboy as he passed by, Shana crossed over to the waitress to give her instructions, then retreated back to the hostess table. She paused only for a moment to look over her shoulder at her father. The smile was tired around the edges, but nonetheless, it glowed with a great deal of affection.

"You're right," Travis commented. When Shawn eyed him quizzically, he referred to the man's comment in his office. "She takes good care of you."

"A little too much good care if you ask me," Shawn grumbled slightly. "When she's around, I can't have caffeine or even Irish coffee. She won't allow me to have spirits of any kind and, as you just saw, she's put her foot down about really good food." An enigmatic smile curved his mouth as he shook his head. "She doesn't realize that she's closing the barn door after the horses've been stolen." He murmured the last sentence under his breath.

But it was still loud enough for Travis to hear. He watched his client closely. "What do you mean?"

The expression on Shawn's face told him he hadn't realized that he'd said the last part out loud. Instead of a direct answer, he said, "I'll explain everything to you when I bring those papers you asked for."

Which turned a throwaway line into a mystery and left Travis wondering if there was more to Shawn O'Reilly than met the eye.

Shortly thereafter, having shared a strong glass of tea and a very light dessert with Shawn, Travis, his doggie bag tucked under his arm, said his good-byes to his new client and host. But first, he was careful to lavish a sufficient amount of praise regarding the chef's efforts. He made a point of it because the restaurant obviously meant a great deal to Shawn. The praise required no embellishment on his part. Both the quesadilla and the corned beef had been exceptionally tasty.

Travis actually debated calling Trevor when he got home to suggest that his brother pay the restaurant a visit in the near future. The menu might give him some new ideas for his own establishment. Trevor was damn good at creating new dishes, but it never hurt to be open.

Holding his doggie bag, Travis was about to go through the front door when Shana called out to him. As he turned away from the entrance, she came around the front of her desk. She didn't want him leaving with a bad impression of her. Why that mattered so much to her, she wasn't really sure.

But it did.

Reaching him, she placed her hand on his arm, as if to anchor his attention. "You probably think I'm a bully."

The very notion made him grin. "Trust me," he told her. "'Bully' is probably the last term I would apply to you."

He noticed a blush rise to her cheeks. Again, it felt to him as if she was delving into his mind, reading his thoughts. Seeing the attraction he was trying to bank down for professional reasons.

Travis recalled hearing stories about people from ancient cultures in both Ireland and Scotland who claimed to have "the gift" or "the sight." In modern terms, it was now referred to as clairvoyance.

Shana would have made one beautiful fortune teller, he thought.

Despite his dismissal of her behavior, she still wanted him to understand and not think of her as a control freak or, worse, a shrew.

"It's just that Dad's eaten whatever he wanted to all his life, but not without consequences. His cardiologist wants him to cut back on the fried foods and fats. He's already had a couple of angioplasties." Shana automatically began to explain the term. "That's when—"

"I know what an angioplasty is," he told her.

"Sorry, I didn't mean to insult you. It's just that a lot of people have heard the term but don't know what it entails. I didn't until Dad started having chest pains and I forced him to see a specialist. After the treadmill, the doctor insisted he immediately go across the street to the hospital to have the procedure done. He actually pulled rank to commandeer an operating room on the spot. Dad had to have another angioplasty the following month when the first one collapsed. The second one, thank God, took."

She closed her eyes for a second, remembering how worried she'd been, sitting in that waiting room, watching the operating room door for any sign of the surgeon. It felt as if the procedure had taken forever.

Shana flushed ruefully. "My father means a great deal to me, and I just want to keep him around as long as possible. If it takes confiscating his dinner once in a while, I'm up to it. Anything to keep him healthy—or reasonably so," she amended.

"I'm the last one you have to explain yourself to, Shana," he assured her. "My family means a great deal to me, too."

"My father *is* my whole family," she told him.

"Your father mentioned a sister. Susan."

She shrugged. The peasant blouse dipped enticingly. He did his best to keep his eyes on her face. "I have no idea where she is. I haven't seen her for at least a couple of years."

"At your mother's funeral?" he guessed.

She nodded, then pushed the memory away. "How big is your family, Mr. Marlowe?"

"I'll only answer that if you call me Travis."

She inclined her head. "All right, Travis. How big is your family?"

"I've got three brothers and a sister," Travis told her.

She tried to imagine what that would be like, to have siblings to talk to. To argue with and love. Had to be nice. By the time she was old enough to try to get to know Susan, her sister was out of the house, returning only when she needed money or a temporary place to stay between trysts.

"Younger? Older?" she asked.

Since he didn't seem to be leaving just yet, Travis thought it prudent to move away from the entrance. Stepping to the side out of the way of incoming traffic, he answered her question. "My sister Kelsey is the baby of the family, and I've got one older brother, Mike."

She made the natural assumption. "Then the other two are younger?"

There was a county-wide power outage the night they were born. Approximate time and order of their births were recorded. "Only by minutes, although that has been up for discussion more than once."

She was quiet for a moment, then looked at him in surprise as she made the only logical connection. "That makes you—"

"—One of triplets," Travis completed.

He was accustomed to people being either surprised

or a tad skeptical, as if they thought he was pulling their leg. A delighted smile was definitely something out of the realm of his expectations.

"Triplets?" she echoed, her face lighting up. "Knew there was something unique about you."

"On the contrary," Travis deadpanned. "I look exactly like these two other guys."

She liked his sense of humor. He didn't take himself seriously like Jacob, her father's accountant who, as far as she knew, was physically incapable of smiling. It helped having someone like Travis guiding them through the grim territory of wills and living trusts. She hated even thinking about that. She'd only gone along with her father's insistence to see a lawyer because it seemed to mean so much to him.

Shana had always thought of herself as practical. But focusing on her father's will was a little *too* practical. She didn't like the way it centered her attention on the time when her father would no longer be with her. She didn't want his money, or the house, or the restaurant. All she wanted was him.

What was it like to have two other people somewhere with your face?

"I'd like to see that for myself someday," she told him.

His first thought was to invite her and her father over to his parents' house for one of Kate's Sunday dinner gatherings. The fact that it did occur to him took him by surprise. He'd never wanted to invite any of his other clients to the house.

Definitely needed some sleep, he counseled himself.

But since she had expressed an interest in seeing him with his brothers, he decided to do the next best thing.

"Just a second."

Shifting the doggie bag under his arm, he reached into his back pocket for his wallet. The billfold was worn and creased, as well as permanently curved from having assumed the shape of his body for several years now. He'd gotten the wallet while in college to take the place of the one that had literally fallen apart. This one would have to suffer the same fate before he bought a new one.

Opening the wallet, he flipped through several photographs, most of them as worn as the leather that surrounded them.

"Here it is," he announced, turning the wallet around so that she could see the photograph. It was of four blond-haired boys, beaming as they all stood around a baby.

She smiled and studied the photograph more closely. The wallet felt warm against her fingers, and something stirred inside her.

"I take it you were all a little younger then."

He laughed and nodded. "That was at Kelsey's christening."

"You don't have anything a little more recent?" she prodded, handing the wallet back to him.

He thought of Trevor's wedding. Kate and Bryan had gone all out and hired two photographers as well as someone to film the entire ceremony and reception. He recalled posing for several "official" wedding photographs with the family.

"Actually, yes, I do," he told her, tucking the wallet back in his pocket, "but not with me."

She found herself intrigued and curious. "Maybe you'll have it with you when we come by the office on Thursday."

He could do that, he thought. "Sure, no problem. I just have to find where I put them," he confessed. He'd meant to organize the photographs in an album, along with the ones of Mike's wedding. He thought about the line about the road to hell and good intentions. That described his life, to a T. "I'm definitely not as organized as I'd like to be."

She liked his smile, she thought. It was self-deprecating and unassuming.

"Who is these days? Seems like everything's in fast-forward." She glanced over her shoulder. As had happened earlier, there were people gathering around the hostess desk again. "Well, I'd better get back to work before they decide to go somewhere else."

"Business seems to be pretty good," he commented.

"The food's excellent here, but it's Dad who makes the difference. He likes to float from table to table, making everyone feel at home. He spends most of his time every evening mingling with the guests, making them feel as if they were family." She shook her head. "It helps to keep his mind off Susan."

"I thought you said she wasn't around."

"That's exactly the point. She's not. But Dad can't help being Dad. He's worries about her, where she is, what's she's doing, if she's all right. It's just the way he is," she explained. And then, because he was an outsider and no matter what else she was, Susan was still family, she covered for her. "My sister's not a bad person. She just has these demons...she's always falling for someone who isn't right for her, almost as if she's trying to punish herself for something. Trouble is, she winds up punishing Dad because he cares so much."

Shana stopped abruptly, afraid that she'd already said far too much.

"You have the kind of face that makes people want to talk to you." She touched his arm lightly again, as if cementing their bond. "See you Thursday."

"I'll be looking forward to it," he told her as he finally went out the door.

Rarely had he ever meant anything more.

Chapter 6

"**M**r. O'Reilly's here." Bea's disembodied voice came over the intercom Thursday at noon.

Travis brushed a stray speck from his jacket, trying not to pay attention to the fact that his pulse started to beat faster. Despite all his efforts to the contrary, Shana had been on his mind—and infiltrated his dreams—for the last two days.

"Send them in," he instructed. It wasn't until a half beat later that he realized the secretary had mentioned only his client, not the man's daughter.

By then, Bea was talking again. "No 'them,' Mr. Marlowe," the woman corrected. "Just him."

As if to underscore Bea's statement, at that moment the heavyset, jovial O'Reilly walked into his office.

"Here I am, just like we agreed."

"Good morning, Mr. O'Reilly." Travis rose from behind his desk. Crossing the room, he shook Shawn's hand and motioned him to the sofa. He glanced hopefully behind his client, but there was no one else there, or in the reception area. Disappointment instantly wove itself through him. He did his best to hide it. "Shana isn't with you?"

"She'll be along," Shawn promised. "I sent her home to pick up the deed to the house." The man opened his briefcase and took out a stack of papers. He offered them to Travis. "Seems I forgot it in the study."

Something in the man's voice caught Travis's attention. Accepting the legal papers, Travis sat down next to his client. "You didn't forget the deed, did you?"

"It's on the desk in the study," Shawn answered evasively. And then he smiled and shook his head. "But no, I didn't forget it. I left it there on purpose," he confirmed. And even that had taken a little sleight of hand to accomplish. "Not an easy thing to do when you have a young woman guarding you like a hawk."

That hadn't been his impression the other evening. Shana had been watchful, but she hadn't devoted her attention to the man exclusively.

Curious, Travis asked, "Why would she feel she needs to guard you?"

"I fell a year ago," Shawn explained. "Didn't break anything except for my pride, but Shana's afraid I'll do it again and this time, she figures I might not be so lucky."

That made sense, Travis thought. And then he got

down to the real question. "Why did you leave the deed at home, Mr. O'Reilly?"

Shawn smiled into his chins. "So I could send her back to fetch it. If I asked her to step out so that I could talk to you alone, she'd be suspicious. I'd have no peace until she wormed it out of me."

The man would have made a good lawyer, Travis couldn't help thinking. He obviously liked to talk. "Wormed what out of you?"

Shawn grew a little more serious. "What I'm about to tell you."

Travis leaned over and lifted the frosted silver pitcher he'd had Bea set out. Very carefully, he poured out two glasses of ice water, and then handed the first to Shawn.

"And it's something you don't want her to know."

Shawn sighed quietly. "She'll find out eventually, but hopefully, not while I'm alive." He flushed slightly and paused to take a long sip from the glass that had been passed to him. "She might not forgive me once she finds out and I really couldn't bear that. I wasn't the one who wanted to keep it from her." He placed the glass back down.

It was obvious to Travis that regret gnawed away at the older man. He waited quietly for the man to go on at his own pace.

"That was my wife's call," Shawn said as he continued. "And, with each year that passed, it became more and more of a burden, and more and more of a bone of contention." He blew out a breath as he shook his head. "Shana should have been told years ago. By my wife," he emphasized, "who was always so good with her. Grace would have made her understand." His eyes were full of contrition. "And not hold it against us."

"Shana's adopted?" Travis guessed.

He couldn't think of anything else that might arouse such concern, such reluctance. Adoption was always a hard matter to approach and it only became more so with each year that went by. With the passage of time, it wasn't the adoption itself that became a sore subject, but the fact that it was kept a secret for years.

"Yes," Shawn admitted after a beat, then added, "in a manner of speaking." He looked uncertain as to how to continue. These particular words did not come easily to him. "But it's not exactly what you think."

Travis waited for the man to continue. When he didn't, Travis didn't push. The man was obviously ready to "confess," to rid himself of the weight he'd been carrying around for the duration of Shana's existence.

Although it was just the two of them in the room, Shawn leaned in closer as he lowered his voice. "Anything I tell you here today doesn't get out, right? It's just between the two of us."

Travis nodded. "Just between the two of us," he echoed, then, to further set the man's mind at ease, he specified. "Our conversation is bound by the attorney-client privilege."

"You wouldn't tell Shana?" Shawn pressed, desperate for reassurance. "I mean, she is part of all this." He waved his hand in a circle to include the documents he'd just brought and, Travis assumed, the living trust he wanted set up.

"Yes, but you're the one retaining my services. That makes you my client and it entitles you to privacy. You can tell me anything and I can't, and *won't* repeat it," Travis told him.

Shawn still needed convincing. "What if Shana becomes your client? What then?"

"It still holds," Travis said. "You're separate people, separate cases. What she tells me in confidence I can't tell you and what you say under those circumstances I can't tell her." He added a coda. "Unless you want me to."

"Oh God, no." Shawn's laugh had no humor to it. "I don't want her to hate me."

The words made Travis think of another scenario, a theme and variation of the first and one that might arouse a sense of guilt in the man. "Is she your daughter, Mr. O'Reilly?"

"Legally and in my heart," Shawn told him with feeling.

Travis shook his head. "No, I mean, is Shana the result of an affair?"

The look on Shawn's face told him that he'd guessed right.

The admission obviously weighed heavily on him, causing the older man's words to emerge slowly and with far less enthusiasm than was his custom.

Shawn had been carrying around the secret with him for a very long time and while he really wanted to rid himself of the burden, it was hard just releasing it at will.

"Yes," Shawn finally answered, "she is. But the affair wasn't mine."

Travis looked at the man in surprise. "Your wife had the affair?"

"Hell, no." Shawn snorted with feeling. "I married a really beautiful woman, boy, and I'm proud to say she was as faithful to me as the day was long. Even when I didn't deserve it," he added with a touch of remorse. The next moment, it was gone. "No, the one who had the affair—if you could call it that—more like a one-night stand that went on for a week—was my daughter." Then, in case there was any doubt, Shawn added, "Susan."

Travis hadn't expected this twist. "Susan is Shana's mother?"

"Yes." The single word dripped with heartache, even after all this time.

Travis tried to wrap his mind around the implications. "That would make you—"

Shawn's snow-white head bobbed up and down. "Her grandfather, not her father, yes." A heavy sigh accompanied the words. "My wife wanted to protect Susan. She also wouldn't hear of her terminating the pregnancy or giving the baby up for adoption. She was very family oriented, my wife. She told Susan that if she had the baby, we would take care of everything, including her."

A melancholy smile twisted his lips. Travis could tell how sad it made him, admitting to his daughter's shortcomings. "Susan was only sixteen at the time and smart enough to know she had no place to go, even though she threatened to run off with that no-good bum who got her pregnant." Another short, humorless laugh preceded his words. "Lucky for us, he disappeared early in the game. Seems he 'didn't know' she was underage. Anyway, Shana was born and we adopted her. Because she insisted, I promised my wife I'd never tell anyone the real story and I never did—until now."

He paused and looked at Travis for a long moment, his eyes searching the younger man's face. "What you do with the information I just gave you is up to you," he continued. "All I ask is that you keep this to yourself until after I'm gone from this earth. I really couldn't bear to have Shana look at me any other way than she does now. It would kill me."

Travis could sympathize with both Shawn and Shana. Shawn had done what he thought was best, trying to protect his granddaughter. But even so, once she found out, Shana would feel betrayed because the person she loved the most had kept such a vital piece of information, of her life, from her. Moreover, finding out her sister was really her mother would undermine the very foundation upon which her life was built, pulling it out from under her.

"Well, hopefully, we won't have to face that eventuality for a good, long time," Travis told him.

Shawn shook his head. "If you're talking about my health, boy, you might just want to change those adjectives." The man grew even more serious. There was pain in his voice. "I don't have very long, Travis. That's why I wanted to rush this living trust thing along. My doctor said I've got congestive heart failure and the damn thing's progressing at a really fast pace. Shana doesn't know," he added, confirming Travis's suspicions. "So you see, I've got to get all my affairs—so to speak," he said, a slight smile curving the corners of his mouth, "in order—and make sure that someone besides Susan has this information. I don't want Shana to be blindsided by her," he added fiercely.

"You know, as hard as this might be for you, I think you should be the one to tell her." Shawn began to protest, but Travis held his hand up, silently asking to be heard out. "She'd feel less betrayed if it came from you. And eventually, she'll understand why you did it."

Shawn shook his head. "I always thought of myself as a brave man. I'm not afraid of dying. But I'll tell you what I am afraid of. I'm afraid of the look of disappointment in her eyes, boy. Afraid of seeing it and knowing that I was the one who put it there."

How much worse would the words sound coming from a stranger? Or what if she stumbled over the truth herself? She would feel that much more betrayed. "I still think Shana would take it better if it came from you."

"Took what better if it came from you, Dad?" Shana asked cheerfully as she entered.

Both men turned toward her, clearly caught off guard by her entrance. She stopped and looked from her father to the cute lawyer.

Had she interrupted something?

"I'm sorry, should I have knocked?"

"No, this is about you," Shawn said, recovering, his mind working rapidly to construct a plausible statement to back up his words. He decided to go with what he'd planned to ask the lawyer to do when he drew up the living trust.

Shana sat down at her father's other side and opened her large purse. She took out a stamped, slightly yellowed document.

"Here's the deed you wanted. It was just where you said it would be." Shana placed it on the coffee table in front of her father, then raised her eyes to his face. "Even though it was supposed to have been in your briefcase," she added tactfully, nodding at the case on the table. "Like I asked you if it was when we left the house."

Broad, squat shoulders moved beneath the jacket. "I'm an old man, Shana. I forget things." His expression was baleful. "What can I say?"

"Don't give me that," she chided. "You are *not* an old man, Dad," she said with affection. "No more than I am. You just pretend to be one when it suits you." Glancing at her father's lawyer, she knew she wouldn't get anything out of him. The man was paid to keep his mouth sealed. So, she went back to the source and leveled her gaze at her father.

"Now, what is it that's about me?" she prodded. When he eyed her blankly, she played along. "What you were talking about with Travis when I walked in."

Stalling, Shawn O'Reilly was the face of innocence. "Oh, that."

He didn't fool her for a moment. He might have had some bouts with illnesses, but the man's mind was as razor sharp as ever.

"Yes, 'that.'"

In his mind, Shawn finalized something he'd been contemplating for the last two days after a great deal of soul searching. "I was just telling Travis here that I've changed my mind about the living trust." He drew himself up. "I'm not going to divide everything equally between you and Susan."

"Oh?" This was the first she'd heard of it. Shana looked at him in surprise.

Travis nearly did the same thing. At the last moment, he managed to keep himself in check. Until O'Reilly had said that, he'd just assumed that the man was gathering his courage together to make a clean breast of it and tell Shana the truth.

Since her father wasn't elaborating, Shana turned to Travis for an explanation. "What did he say he wanted to do?"

Not sure where this was going, Travis passed the ball back to his client. "Why don't you let him tell you?" he suggested. He was careful to avoid calling Shawn her father. The less deliberate reference to that, the better.

Patiently, she turned her eyes back to her father. "Dad?"

Shawn took a breath and began. "Well, darlin', I know a father's supposed to love his kids equally, but I'm only human, not some angel. You've been the one who's always been here for me. You're the one who changed her life around when I had that thing with my heart five years ago—"

"Your heart attack," she supplemented, calling a spade a spade.

"That" was the only way Shawn would acknowledge the incident. "And you're the one who was there to help me when Grace died." He took her hand in his. She was a good girl, he thought. And as such, she'd resist what he had to say. But now that he'd decided, he wasn't about to be talked out of it. "You're the one who's been my rock, Shana. It wouldn't be fair to give you the same amount that Susan gets. Susan hasn't been here for me, not once."

Shana shook her head. This wasn't right. She didn't want Susan's share. She didn't want any of it. She just wanted her father to continue the way he had, for years to come.

"Dad, she's your daughter, same as me."

"But she doesn't act the same as you," he pointed out.

Shana wasn't comfortable with this decision. Although she and Susan had been estranged for a number of years and she resented the way her sister ignored their father, Susan was still her sister, still his daughter. She knew how hurt she would have been if the situation was reversed. She thought back to a time when she'd idolized her sister. The latter never had time for her, but that still didn't change the love that she felt.

"Dad, are you really sure that you want to do something so drastic?"

"I'm sure." He patted her hand. "I want you to know how much I love you."

Her father had grown up poor. As a young man, he'd struggled for every dollar he made, judiciously investing it into his business until it flourished. To him, money meant a great deal.

It didn't to her.

"I know that, Dad," she told him gently, trying to make him understand. "I don't need money to tell me that."

He thought for a moment. There was a practical side to this that he had to make her understand. "Okay, let me put it to you this way. If I split the restaurant between you, give you each half, what do you think Susan would want to do with her half?"

It didn't even take her a second to think about the question. Susan went through money like water. The only time she turned up was when she ran out of it and needed more.

"Sell it."

"Exactly. And you don't have enough money to buy her share," he pointed out, "so it'll go on the market to be sold to whoever makes the best bid. Some stranger will own and run the restaurant I poured my life's blood into," he told her with passion. "I don't want that. Same with the house. You were born in that house, Shana. Grace died in that house." The house was over fifty years old. Sturdy, but old-fashioned by today's tastes. It stood on a nice sized plot which had tremendous appeal in this day of postage-sized yards. "I don't want some stranger tearing down the walls and changing things around. I want you to have it because you made my life—our lives—your mother's and mine—such a pleasure."

Shana blinked, trying to physically push back the tears that were making her lashes heavy. "Dad," she began to protest.

She saw that familiar stubborn look enter Shawn's crystal-blue eyes. "No, I've made up my mind."

Apparently on the spur of the moment, Travis couldn't help thinking.

Shawn turned toward him. "This is what I want, Travis," he told him. "I want only a small amount of one of the bank accounts to go to Susan. I haven't decided how much yet. But the bulk of the accounts, the restaurant and the house, I want that to all go to Shana when I die."

It was a simple enough matter to arrange. "We could leave that one bank account out, not specify it in the terms of the living trust. That way, only Shana's name would appear in the paperwork. It's a little less harsh than having to spell out that you want none of the proceeds to go to Susan. We're making the trust revocable instead of irrevocable. That way, if you change your mind later, your decision can be reversed."

Shawn thought it over for a moment, then nodded. "We'll do it your way," he agreed, "and leave the account out. But I *do* want it spelled out that Susan's not to get any part of the items that are covered under the living trust." Susan was devious, she always had been. He didn't want her tying things up and keeping Shana from what she was entitled to.

"Dad—" Shana began to protest again.

He wasn't about to allow himself to be talked out of it. Shana had a good heart, but Susan didn't. If the situation were reversed, Susan wouldn't have spent a single moment worrying about the fairness of the arrangement, she would have urged him to put it in writing.

"No, Shana, this is for the best, trust me. Someday, you'll understand why I did this."

He was doing it out of a sense of atonement, Travis thought. He didn't like to interfere in his clients' decisions, but in part he was being paid for his judgment and he needed to exercise it. "Mr. O'Reilly, this really might not be the way to go. Maybe you'd like to think it over for a while."

"I have thought it over for a while," Shawn told him. "A long while. And I'm fine with the decision. It's the right thing to do," he said confidently. "And it's what I want."

And that was that.

Chapter 7

Travis hadn't been practicing his profession nearly as long as the other attorneys in the firm. But during his relatively short run, he'd been exposed to his share of clients who displayed less than sterling attributes. The lure of an inheritance—or the withholding of one—brought out the baser instincts and emotions, with greed leading the charge.

So it took him by surprise when Shana leaned over and asked, "Can I override his wishes?" the moment that O'Reilly left the room.

For the better part of the last hour, he and Shawn had been going over the various documents regarding his various bank accounts—both personal and business—his restaurant and the house where he lived with Shana.

The latter had given up her apartment a little more than a year ago, moving back in with O'Reilly to take care of him after he'd suffered a second heart attack. Concerned about yet another recurrence, she never got around to moving out again.

"Well, I think that does it," Travis said. "I'll just have Bea revise the trust, make copies of all of these and you can be on your way." He buzzed the administrative assistant who, rather than answer, just appeared in his doorway. Travis crossed to her. "Bea, I need one copy made of each of these. Plus, these changes to the trust. And the property funding the trust will need to be set out as an exhibit thereto, if you don't mind."

The expression on the woman's face said that of course she did, but that she would do it anyway. Taking the documents from him, Bea turned on her short, squat heel to make a pilgrimage first to the copy machine.

"Wait up, young lady," Shawn called out to Bea, who hadn't heard the description applied to herself for close to half a century. "Mind pointing out the men's room to me?" he asked.

The moment he crossed the threshold, Shana turned and posed her question to Travis.

He wasn't sure that he followed her. "What do you mean?"

"If...if he dies." Travis noticed that she didn't say "when" but "if." He realized that O'Reilly had managed to keep some things from her despite her zeal for being hands-on in her care of him. "Do I have to abide by his wishes?"

Once the terms of the trust had been met and Shawn passed away, the things included beneath the virtual umbrella were hers to do with as she saw fit. "What is it that you'd want to do?" he asked, curious.

"Divide the property equally between us. Susan and me," she added. There was no other family, No nieces or nephews or distant cousins, several times removed. There was just Susan and her. Susan had been married several times—twice or three times if the ceremony by the Tibetan recluse was legitimate—but there were no children.

Travis tried to guess at her reasoning in light of the little he knew about her. "Don't you think you deserve to get more than she does?"

Shana raised her eyes to his. He found he couldn't read them. "Because I'm taking care of him?"

He was a firm believer that good deeds should be rewarded. "That, and because, as he said, you're there for him when he needs you. It's not just little children who need love," Travis said. "Older people need it, too."

"There is no age limit on love," Shana responded. "I know that. But that also means that Susan would be very hurt if she knew that Dad decided not to give her the same amount he was giving me. My sister has very low self-esteem as it is. Why else would she keep throwing her lot in with men who are only out to use her?"

That question fell more into Trent's realm than his, Travis thought. Or Kate's. "I take it you don't believe in the old adage about reaping what you've sown."

"Susan's life is hard. I don't like her neglecting Dad this way, but she's never really been able to get her act together. Under all that anger and confusion, there's a really good person there."

She actually believed that, he thought. That much he could see in her eyes. "Maybe being left out in the cold, so to speak, might do her some good. It could be a real wake-up call for Susan."

She looked disappointed with his answer. "Then you agree with my father?"

He didn't know enough yet to really agree or disagree, although he did have leanings based on the information O'Reilly had shared with him earlier today.

Since she was waiting for an answer, he skirted the issue. "I think that a person has the right to distribute his assets the way he sees fit. Although it would be nice to believe, we are *not* all created equal. We're just created with the right to *try* to be equal." He'd do her one better. "Everyone thinks that a parent is supposed to love all their children the same. But each kid is different and, being human, parents react differently to them. I'm sure that Mr. O'Reilly bailed Susan out—figuratively—more than once, but he just wants to reward you for not taking after her."

Shana frowned at the implication. "I'm not doing any of this to be 'rewarded.'"

"All the more reason why you should be," Travis pointed out. "Because you're doing what you're doing—going out of your way—selflessly."

She looked at him for a long moment, putting her own interpretation to his words. "Then you'd give me a hard time about it?" she wanted to know. "When the time comes and I want to give Susan half of everything, you'll try to stop me?"

"I can't stop you," he said honestly.

Did she have any idea how appealing she was? He found himself more and more mesmerized by her, more focused on the way her lips moved when she spoke. He had to get a grip. On himself, and not her, he added, struggling to bank down the desire to touch her, to frame her face with his hands, to breathe in her perfume and to lose himself in the silkiness of her hair.

"But I would ask you to reconsider your impulse and not do anything hasty. I'd ask you to take a cooling off period. There's a reason for everything and Mr. O'Reilly would want you to consider all sides of this."

His wording puzzled her. What sides were there beyond what was so apparent? "You're making this sound very mysterious."

Travis drew back from the subject. "Sorry, that wasn't my intention." He saw Shawn entering the room, followed by Bea who placed the originals and the photocopies she'd made on his desk side by side along with multiple original trust documents. Travis gave up a silent prayer of thanksgiving as he rose to his feet again. Saved by the cavalry. "Mr. O'Reilly, you're just in time to review and sign all the papers. The Exhibit thereto, noting all trust property documented today, we will prepare shortly."

Barely hearing him, Shawn forced a smile to his lips as he took a seat again. "Bring them on."

Shana was immediately concerned. When she took Shawn's hand in hers, it was clammy.

"Dad, are you all right?" She looked at his face. He'd lost his color, and there was a line of perspiration on his brow. "You look very pale."

Shawn waved away her concern, struggling to center himself. His strength returned in slow dribbles and drabs. "Just lost my breath there for a minute," he admitted.

Shana and Travis exchanged looks. "Do you want me to take you to the hospital?" Travis offered. He was on his feet before the man answered.

Shawn caught hold of his arm, tugging Travis back down to his seat. "If I went to the hospital every time I lost my breath, I would have never left the ER parking lot for the last two years. I'm all right. Really," he emphasized when he saw the doubtful expression on Shana's face. "Now, where are those papers you said you want me to sign?"

Travis presented him with the short stack and handed him a pen. After Travis pointed out the major trust provisions, Shawn began writing his signature in the appropriate place.

Shana remained unconvinced. "Dad, maybe I should call Dr. Darel—"

Shawn shook his head, stopping her. "I just saw him last week," he reminded her.

That didn't deter Shana. "Well, you can just see him again."

His voice was soft, but he remained firm. "I'd rather see the restaurant. That always makes me feel good."

Why couldn't she get him to listen? Was he determined to run himself into the ground? "Dad—"

"Shana, stop fussing," he ordered. Finished, Shawn pushed the pile of papers closer to Travis on the coffee table. "Anything else to sign?" he asked him.

Travis gathered all the pages together, straightening them into a neat pile. "No, that was the last of them." He clipped them all together. "I'll begin funding the trust and should have the official copies for you shortly."

Shawn looked well pleased. "That fast?"

"You're paying premium rates," Travis reminded him. "You're entitled to premium service."

Shawn beamed, his eyes crinkling into small blue slits. "I like the way you think, boy. Come by the restaurant tonight." Leaning on Shana, he rose heavily to his feet, then clapped Travis on the shoulder. "I'll have the chef make something special for you."

"Thanks, but there's really no need for that," Travis protested.

"Sure there is," Shawn countered in that "don't-argue-with-me-boy" voice. "You're going to be explaining all the finer points of this trust to me. Singin' for your supper, so to speak," he added with a broad wink.

Travis laughed, shaking his head. "Well, since you put it that way, how can I refuse?"

Shawn looked pleased. Some of the color was returning to his face. "You can't."

Was it his imagination, or had the man glanced at his daughter first before silently declaring his maneuver a triumph? No, it was probably his imagination, Travis decided.

Shawn took a deep breath, then let it out slowly. Releasing her arm, he made his way to the door. "All right, Shana, I think I'll stop at the house before going to the restaurant."

She was beside him in two steps. "I knew it. You *are* feeling sick."

He'd thought of something he might have forgotten to include within the trust's protective cover. "No, I want to check something out before going into work."

She didn't believe him for a second. He was going to go to his room and lie down for a few minutes, she'd bet anything on it.

One hand fisted at her waist, she eyed him suspiciously. "What?"

Instead of answering her, he glanced over his shoulder at Travis. "Don't have kids, Travis. They turn on you the second they're out of diapers."

But it was obvious to anyone who listened or looked that there was a great deal of affection in the man's voice as well as in his eyes when he regarded Shana.

"Sometimes, even before," Shana added, winking at Travis.

"I'll take that into consideration," Travis promised as he closed the door.

He had ten minutes until his next appointment. It would take him that long to talk his pulse down to a manageable level.

"Trav, what are you doing tonight?"

He'd picked up the phone automatically. Bea had

ducked out for two hours right after lunchtime, muttering something about a dental appointment and a root canal. That had left him on his own, fielding the next two clients by himself. The second one had just left and he was pulling papers together, mentally outlining tomorrow when the phone rang.

It took Travis a moment to connect the voice on the other end of the line to a face. "Mike?"

"Yeah. What are you doing tonight?" his brother repeated the question.

Tonight. Shana. A warm glow detonated in his abdomen, spreading out like a sunburst. What *was* it about that woman that transformed him from a competent attorney to a bowl of gelatin? He didn't know, but he definitely wanted to find out.

"Actually, I'm going out."

Mike laughed. "On a school night?"

Was he that predictable? He supposed he was. He usually didn't go out during the week. Like Trevor, he found himself working long hours and forgetting about the time.

"Very funny."

"This thing you've got tonight, can you get out of it?" Mike asked.

He caught himself smiling. Moreover, he couldn't seem to stop. "It's not exactly something I want to get out of."

"Oh." It was a long, pregnant "oh" that seemed to go on for several seconds before he added, "Then bring her along."

"What makes you think there's a 'her'?"

He heard Mike laugh. "Elementary, my dear Watson. Because you didn't flat out say there wasn't."

Because he judged the feelings he was experiencing as coming under the heading of adolescent, Travis preferred not to share this with his older brother. "This involves a client."

Mike sounded pleased at the information. "All the better. Reschedule."

Not on your life. "And just why would I want to do that?"

He heard Mike blow out a breath. "Because I'm trying to get the family together, Trav. We're all meeting at Dad and Kate's house tonight at eight. Everyone else already said yes."

No pressure here, Travis thought. "Again, why?"

Mike was being deliberately evasive. "If I wanted you to know now, I'd tell you now. The purpose behind meeting tonight is to tell you tonight. All of you at the same time."

Curious, Travis started theorizing out loud. "Okay, you're not announcing you're getting married because you and Miranda are already married—although what that beautiful woman sees in you is beyond my scope of comprehension—and you wouldn't be getting us together to announce you're getting divorced because you wouldn't be sounding so damn cheerful about losing someone like Miranda—" And then it hit him like a ton of bricks. "—Oh my God."

"What?" Mike's voice sounded alert, suspicious—and somewhat crestfallen.

It could only be one thing. "Miranda's pregnant, isn't she?"

He heard Mike take in a deep breath, as if bracing himself. "I'm neither going to confirm nor deny that. You want an answer, you show up at Dad's house tonight at eight."

He was right. He'd bet a year's salary on it. Especially since Mike wasn't flatly denying it. That was as good as an admission any day.

"You son of a gun. What about all this talk about waiting five years, putting together more of a nest egg before you even *thought* about having kids?" Travis threw Mike's own words back at him.

Mike relented. Partially. "All you really need is the nest," he admitted with a laugh. "You tell anyone else and I'll have your head on a platter," Mike threatened.

Travis laughed. "Oh, like nobody else is going to figure this out."

"Just show up tonight—and act surprised if you know what's good for you," Mike instructed. "Oh, and bring your 'client' along."

He wasn't quite sure he liked the way Mike said that. "Why would you want me to do that?"

"Because, Trav, I want to meet the woman who's piqued your interest, that's why."

Habit had him being defensive. He didn't appreciate being read like a book, not by his brothers. He made allowances for Kate. "Who said anything about her piquing my interest?"

"It's there in your voice, Trav. Listen to yourself

sometime. And, for God's sake, just be happy and be content with that. The guys and I were beginning to think you're studying to be a hermit in your off-hours. See you tonight." Not waiting for a response, Mike hung up.

Travis sat there for a moment, just holding the receiver in his hand, thinking.

Several minutes went by. And then Bea came in. "I'm back," she announced, a slight lisp due to her numb lower lip accompanying her words. Her small eyes narrowed as she appraised him. There was no attempt to veil her annoyance. "You going to sit there, making love to your receiver all afternoon or do you plan to work for a living?"

He hung up the phone. "You can be replaced, you know."

"No, I can't," she retorted glibly and with confidence. "Your three o'clock is here." With that, she turned back around. There was a defiant swing to her hips as she left the office.

Travis grinned to himself. He was going to be an uncle. Who'd've thunk it?

During his last appointment he had been engaged in a mental game of tennis, going back and forth as to his course of action.

He knew he had to cancel. Not to seem rude and he didn't want to offend O'Reilly. The man would be expecting him to show up at the restaurant. It had been almost a mandate.

His attendance at Mike's little impromptu gathering

went without saying. Even though he was absolutely certain he'd guessed the reason behind the meeting, he wasn't about to deprive his sister-in-law of the joy of making the announcement. That's just the way things were.

You trained us well, Kate, he thought.

What gave him pause was that he wanted to ask Shana to come with him. He was fairly sure her father would find someone to cover for her at work. And since, technically, she wasn't his client, which meant there really wasn't a conflict of interest at play here, he was free to ask her.

He *wanted* to ask her.

The only thing stopping him was that he didn't know what would come next. What he felt right now was stronger than anything he'd ever experienced, even with the woman he'd been engaged to. That in itself was pretty unnerving.

He didn't like being unnerved.

He liked knowing what every step was all about before he ever ventured to take it.

But this was different.

This was the unknown. There were no security blankets at play here.

He glanced at the five-by-six-inch photograph on his desk. It was taken when he and his brothers were six and seven. At his father's wedding to Kate. But he looked beyond the photograph, to the reflection that hovered over it. His reflection.

"Afraid?" he challenged the reflection.

The next moment, he was reaching for the phone.

He'd started to dial the area code before he realized he didn't know the number to the restaurant. Stopping, he leafed through the packet of papers Shawn had left with him until he found it.

The voice that answered the phone was hers. He'd know it anywhere.

Travis did his best to sound businesslike. He didn't succeed too well. "Shana? It's Travis. Would your father mind if you took the evening off?"

There was a pause. Good pause? Bad pause? He couldn't tell.

"No, he's been after me to take some time off for a while now. Says I'm cutting into his space. What did you have in mind?"

"My older brother is holding an impromptu family meeting. I can't get out of it."

"I see."

How did he approach this without making it sound as if he was getting serious about her? How could he be getting serious about her when they hadn't even gone out? What the hell had come over him?

"I'd like to bring you with me."

There was a long pause on the other end. Just as he was about to ask if she was still there, he heard her say, "All right." His heart jumped. *Idiot.* "What time?"

"Same time I was going to come to your restaurant. Eight. I can swing by and pick you up at seven-thirty," he told her.

"Sounds like a plan to me. Come to the restaurant. I'll be waiting."

"Great."

He vaguely heard himself say "Goodbye." The receiver slid from his fingers as he broke the connection, landing in the cradle with a clatter. A single refrain drummed through his brain.

I'll be waiting.

Chapter 8

Ordinarily, Travis wasn't the type to do things on a whim. Of all the Marlowe men, he had become the most steadfast one, even more so than his father. He was the one who always thought things through carefully before acting. The role of a family lawyer suited him to a tee.

Friendly, warm and outgoing, he still could not be called flamboyant.

Like all of them, Travis had been affected by his mother's death, by her abrupt and permanent absence from his life coming after five years of a daily relationship. Even now, more than twenty-two years later, his mother's death affected the way he approached all relationships—warily. Not at first, but if anything semi-serious seemed to be in the offing, he always rethought his feelings.

Which was why everyone in the family was surprised when they discovered that he was bringing someone to a family gathering. Other than Adrianne, who'd lasted only a short while, he'd never done that before. For the most part, when he dated, which was not frequently, he'd always kept his dating life separate from his family life. That he'd only known Shana O'Reilly for a time equal to the longevity of a fruit fly, just added to the overall mystery.

His family weren't the only people who were surprised by his sudden change in behavior.

So was he.

Yet here he was, standing before the door of Shawn's Li'l Bit of Heaven, about to go in and shake things up in what had, heretofore, been his well-ordered life.

He had his hand over the door handle, but he couldn't make himself open the door.

"In or out, buddy," a deep, gravelly voice behind him prodded impatiently.

"Exactly what I was thinking," Travis confessed, more to himself than the irritated, would-be patron.

Making up his mind, Travis pulled the door open and stepped inside the restaurant. The man behind him elbowed him out of the way and strode toward the hostess table, muttering something unflattering regarding people who couldn't make up their minds.

Shana was waiting for him.

She had been for the last half hour, her gaze drawn to the door every time it opened and someone entered. And each time she would look, something tightened inside of her in anticipation.

The same way it did whenever the phone on her desk rang tonight.

One was in anticipation of seeing him walk through the doorway, the other in anticipation of Travis calling to cancel his plans after all.

She wasn't altogether sure which one she was rooting for.

Until she saw him walk in.

The way her heart raced before she took a deep, calming breath, told her which side had won. Try as she might to be indifferent, she wanted him here more than she didn't.

But even that bothered her.

She hadn't expected to find herself attracted to anyone, not for a good, long while. She thought she had more control over herself than that. It wasn't all that many months ago that she'd given Kevin his walking papers. Kevin, of the wide smile and wider charm. Kevin, who excelled in effortlessly turning a girl's head. Kevin, who thought that he rightly deserved to be the center of any woman's universe. Certainly the center of the woman's who he'd chosen to be his wife.

His glaring flaw had come as a complete surprise to her, arriving without preamble after she'd given him her heart and had seriously begun to envision her life as his wife.

It exploded like a land mine the afternoon he tried to talk her into getting her own apartment again and moving out of her father's house. When she protested that her father still needed to have someone around to help him out, Kevin had frowned and shook his head, like a parent whose child had given the wrong answer to a simple homework question.

"You shouldn't put your life on hold like that," he told her. "Don't get me wrong. Your dad's a nice guy and all that. He's damn lucky, he's got enough money to hire himself a good caretaker—"

"Giver," she'd heard herself correcting Kevin even as a numbness began to creep through her. Squeezing her stomach. Making her ill. "Caregiver."

"Yeah, whatever," Kevin'd dismissed impatiently. "The bottom line is that you don't have to be his prisoner, running every time he needs something."

"I don't run," she protested defensively.

"Looks like running to me," he observed. "It was okay when I was just going out with you. But now I've given you a ring. We're going to get married. Things have to change." She remembered the look in Kevin's eyes as he tendered his ultimatum. He was completely confident of the outcome. "The bottom line is that it's going to be him—or me."

Everything was bottom line to Kevin. It had grown to be his favorite catch phrase, something he repeated at least several times a day, most likely without realizing it, the way some people found themselves trapped within the confines of a mindless phrase like, "you know?"

She fed it back to him.

"The bottom line is that you're a cold, self-centered bastard," she'd told him, angry that he'd placed her in this kind of a position. She knew her father would never do that to her, never make her choose like that. She pulled off the diamond engagement ring Kevin had given her. The one he'd let drop cost over fifteen thousand dollars. It took everything she had not to throw the ring at him the way she wanted to. "I don't know how I missed it all these months."

Stunned, he'd looked at her as if she'd just regressed into a blithering idiot. Grabbing the ring she held out to him, he'd predicted, "You'll be sorry," and stormed out of her life.

"I doubt it," she said quietly to the door he'd slammed in his wake.

And then she cried. Cried because he'd hurt her. Cried because she turned out to be so wrong about him. Cried because the life she'd envisioned had been proven to be a tissue of lies.

She didn't want to cry again. Not because she'd been hurt or disappointed to find out that someone she'd learned to care about wasn't really worth the effort.

As Travis approached her, she promised herself this time was going to different. This time would be strictly fun. With absolutely no strings. Her body might wind up involved in this little venture, but her heart would be tucked away in a safety deposit box, held in reserve for the right man—if such a man existed.

With that resolved, she deliberately ignored the flutter inside her chest cavity, widened her smile and took her purse out from behind the desk.

"Have yourself a good time."

Shana swallowed a gasp. How did a man who tipped the scales at over two hundred pounds, distributed over a relatively short frame, manage to sneak up behind her so quietly? Shana wondered as she swung around to face her father.

He looked good tonight, she thought, pride mingling with a sense of relief. But she still hesitated leaving him. If she hadn't found him when he'd had that second heart attack, he wouldn't be standing here right now. That haunted her, especially in the wee hours of the morning.

"You're sure you'll be all right tonight without me?"

The restaurant owner laughed as he nodded a greeting to Travis. "Hard as it is to believe, baby girl, yeah, I think I can muddle through one night without you. This restaurant has been muddling through way before you were even a gleam in anyone's eye. Now go, have some fun." He leaned over so that only she could hear his words. "He seems like a nice guy. If he's not, tell 'im about my new huntin' knife. The one I use for skinnin' critters."

Suppressing a laugh, Shana shook her head. Her father always twanged when he grew protective of her. When he'd heard the full story about the broken engagement from her, it was all Shana could do to keep him from going out after Kevin to "set him straight" for making her cry. He'd said something about vivisection being involved until she made him swear to forget about it. Kevin, she insisted, wasn't worth the trouble.

"I'll tell him," she promised, kissing the soft cheek. "Now, don't push yourself too hard, you hear me? And if you start feeling tired or weak—"

Shawn nodded and wearily recited, "I'll call you."

She looked at him for a long moment. She knew better. She might be able to get him to say the words, but no way would she get her father to live up to them. "No, you won't."

Shawn turned toward his attorney. "Take this girl off my hands, boy," he implored. "She's got more mothering in her than a hen with a hundred chicks running around her."

"I'll do what I can," Travis told his client. Trying not to seem too eager, he turned his attention to Shana. "Ready?"

Why her stomach would suddenly tighten in response to the look in his eyes, she had no idea. She didn't feel equipped to explore it at the moment. Instead, she forced her smile to remain where it was and nodded as she casually slipped her arm through his.

"Ready."

"Have a good time," Shawn called after them, smiling to himself. From where he stood, things looked very encouraging.

It was nice when life actually went according to plan, he thought.

With any luck...

Shawn didn't finish the thought because it might be bad luck and he had no desire to jinx things.

Rubbing his hands together like a man looking forward to what was to pass, he turned back to the restaurant and the rest of his evening.

"So, you didn't tell me," Shana said as she pulled her seat belt out and slid the metal tongue into the groove.

It clicked into place. "What's this big family gathering all about?"

His own seat belt fastened, Travis put his key into the ignition and turned it. The engine came to life. "It's supposed to be a secret." Looking over his shoulder, he pulled out of the parking space in one smooth motion. "But by process of elimination, I think Mike's wife is pregnant."

She thought for a minute, but was unable to assign Mike a position in the family hierarchy. "Which one is Mike again?"

Travis spared her a grin. He liked that she asked rather than let things float along without clarification. "Mike's the one who isn't a triplet."

She nodded, assimilating the information. It clicked with another piece she'd taken in the other day. "The older one."

"By a whole year," Travis put in. He thought of his earlier conversation with Mike. "By the way, we're supposed to act surprised when they make the announcement."

"Surprised," she repeated, underscoring it with a quick nod of her head. "Got it. I can manage that, seeing as how I'm already surprised."

"By what?"

Easing onto the brake at the red light, he spared her a quick glance. Was it his imagination, or did her perfume fill the inside of his vehicle?

"Your invitation. Most guys don't bring a girl to meet their entire family on a first date."

The light turned. The second it did, someone behind

him leaned on his horn. A choice word rose to Travis's lips, but he swallowed it. Instead, he stepped on the gas, sailing across the intersection.

"Is that what this is?" he asked innocently. "A first date?"

Okay, had she missed a signal? Assumed something that wasn't intended? Embarrassment reared its hoary head, threatening to color everything in shades of red. "Isn't it?"

"I don't know. Maybe," he allowed. "I actually kind of thought of it as being a transferred dinner invitation."

She almost bought it, but then saw the glimmer of a smile on his lips. He was teasing her. Or maybe having as much trouble admitting their attraction as she was.

"If that was the case, why isn't my father sitting next to you instead of me?" she asked, then reminded him, "He was the one who tendered the invitation, I didn't."

Caught, Travis laughed. It was a date all right. He might as well call a spade a spade. "You ever think of becoming a lawyer?"

She shook her head. "Too much memorization. I'd have never passed the bar."

"Then you did think about it."

"For about two minutes," she conceded. "The things I was drawn to weren't practical."

As she said that, she couldn't help thinking of Kevin. Would Travis fall into that category, too? No, she told herself the next moment. Travis wouldn't fall into that category because, as cute as he was, she had no intentions of falling for him.

Fun, that was all this was about. Just fun, nothing more. She deserved a little fun in her life. Fun without consequences.

"Such as?" he asked.

"Art," she told him. "I love to paint, to draw." She couldn't remember a time when she hadn't held a sketch pad and pencil in her hand. Her father had the drawings to prove it. She'd only recently discovered that he had saved every single scribble, every single picture she'd ever put a pencil or brush to. How could she not be devoted to a man like that? "It's not exactly a way to make a living," she admitted. Even though her father would have been willing to underwrite her efforts no matter how long it took for her to succeed.

Luckily for both of them, she was content to keep her artistic leanings within the limits of a hobby and work at the restaurant.

"Do you do much of that?" Travis queried. "Paint?" he added when she didn't answer him right away.

Shana debated telling him. Somehow, it sounded as if she was bragging. But he had asked. So she told him with a careless shrug. "The paintings that hang in the restaurant are all mine."

Her father had not only encouraged her to paint, he'd also insisted on paying her for the paintings. He refused to take any of them as a gift and said just having her around was gift enough.

How could Kevin have expected her to turn her back on someone who loved her so unconditionally? Especially when Kevin was placing conditions on his love

NO POSTAGE
NECESSARY
IF MAILED
IN THE
UNITED STATES

BUSINESS REPLY MAIL
FIRST-CLASS MAIL   PERMIT NO. 717   BUFFALO, NY

POSTAGE WILL BE PAID BY ADDRESSEE

SILHOUETTE READER SERVICE
PO BOX 1867
BUFFALO NY 14240-9952

for her. Or what he perceived as love, she thought. She sincerely regretted that she had ever wasted her time with someone like Kevin.

She slanted a look at Travis. *And what are you like? Under that neatly pressed suit and that warm smile. What are you really like?*

Travis vaguely remembered noticing several paintings adorning the restaurant walls. For the life of him, he couldn't recall a single one of them. He was aware of liking them, but he'd been too focused on Shana to pay attention to anything else.

"I'll have to take a closer look the next time I come by," he told her.

A throwaway line if she'd ever heard one, she thought. Out loud, she said, "You do that" thinking that, in all likelihood, he never would.

The front door to his parents' house was unlocked. Travis knew it would be. Whenever Kate had the family over, she didn't bother locking the door. "Who would want to tangle with the Marlowe men?" she'd ask with a laugh.

"Or Marlowe women," Kelsey always threw in.

Opening the door now, Travis gestured for Shana to walk in ahead of him.

The moment she did, she found herself enfolded in an embrace that exude warmth and the scent of lavender and vanilla.

"Hello, I'm Kate Marlowe," the slender blonde on the other end of the embrace told her half a second before she released her and took a step back.

Caught off guard, it took Shana a moment to recover. The blonde smiled and waited.

"Shana O'Reilly," she finally said. Familiar with the older woman's name, thanks to having grilled Travis, Shana could only stare. She'd grown up thinking all parents were supposed to look weathered rather than youthful. The woman standing before her, making her feel welcomed, seemed more like Travis's sister than his mother. "You're his mother?" she couldn't help asking with no attempt to mask her surprise.

"Still as fantastic looking as the first day I met her," Bryan said as he joined the group by the front door. He slipped his arm around the woman who'd made his life worth living again. "She wears well," he added with a laugh, then put out his hand to her. "Hi, I'm Travis's father, Bryan. You must be Shana."

"I must be," she answered, her smile belying her nervousness.

Travis didn't remember telling Mike her name. Which meant that someone had taken it upon themselves to do a little snooping before he got here. Probably Kelsey, he decided. Threading his fingers through Shana's, he gave her hand a squeeze and then said, "Okay, let's take this hurdle now."

She had no idea what he was referring to.

The next moment, Travis was raising his voice in order to make an announcement. "Everyone, this is Shana O'Reilly. Shana, this is—" Starting with the closest ones to them, he ran through the list of names until he'd named everyone in his family, including his brothers' wives.

The names swarmed around her brain like bees circling their hive. How was she supposed to keep everyone straight?

As if reading her mind, Kate slipped behind her and whispered, "Don't worry, there won't be a quiz at the end of the evening. After a while, you'll get the hang of who's who."

She doubted it, Shana thought. She looked over toward two of the men Travis had identified with his rapid-fire delivery. Granted, they were dressed differently from one another—and Travis—but they were still almost eerily identical.

Travis had introduced them to her as the "other two triplets," Trent and Trevor. She'd stared at them, then looked back at him, searching for something to make him stand apart, other than his clothing. She came up with nothing.

"I'm not too sure about that," she told the older woman.

Kate smiled at her, unfazed. She knew exactly what had to be going through the young woman's mind. Utter confusion. If Shana was to be part of the family, Kate thought confidently, she'd learn quickly enough how to tell the three men apart. In her own case, it had taken her less than a day when she'd first arrived here.

"Don't force it," she advised kindly. "It'll come. You'll see."

"Or, you can always try tagging them, like I did," Kelsey told her, joining the small, all-female circle.

"Tagging them?" Shana asked, curious. "You mean like they do on the Discovery Channel?"

Kelsey nodded. "Something like that. I'd give one of them a bruised arm, punch another in the eye. Helped to keep them straight," she deadpanned.

"She's not kidding." Kate laughed at the stunned expression on Shana's face. "I thought the boys were a handful—until Kelsey came along."

"Sugar and spice and everything nice was definitely *not* a line created to describe Kelsey," Travis told her, returning with two glasses of punch. He handed Shana one before taking a sip from his own.

"Careful, Mister," Kelsey warned, "or I'll tell Shana all your secrets."

Shana grinned. "Tell me anyway."

Kelsey nodded her approval at Shana's response. "I like her, Travis," she told her brother, smiling broadly. "I really do like her."

Shana looked a little embarrassed. Travis laughed shortly, shifting the focus to himself rather than Shana. "Well, I guess I can die happy now."

"No dying," Kate chided. "At least, not before Mike and Miranda make their big announcement."

She slipped one arm through Shana's and the other through Travis's, urging them toward the inner circle that was forming.

In her head, Kelsey was already writing out the announcements. For Travis and the woman he'd brought with him.

Chapter 9

Shana could remember when she'd been a little girl and silently suffered from the latest snub she'd received from Susan. She'd fantasized about what it would be like to be part of a large family. A large, *jovial* family where everyone cared for each other.

It wasn't that she didn't love, or wasn't grateful to, her mother and father. She did, and was. As far as she was concerned, they were wonderful people. But growing up, they also seemed so old to her. Positively ancient in comparison to the parents of the other children in her class. Because they were so much older than she was, her parents couldn't create that young, vital atmosphere she wanted so desperately.

That was where her imaginary family came in. That

family was stuffed to the gills with brothers and sisters who *always* had time for her and always listened to what she had to say. And her imaginary parents were never too tired, never too busy to do whatever it was that she wanted to do.

That imaginary family, Shana now thought, was very much like the one she had met this evening. Travis's family.

Despite the fact that they were all in their twenties, Travis's brothers and sister all teased one another and, once or twice during the course of the evening, he and his brothers ganged up on Kelsey.

But his sister, Shana noted with delight, gave as good as she got, refusing to back down even though she found herself exceedingly outnumbered. It was all in fun, all with love.

That would have been her, Shana thought fondly, if she had been born into this family instead of the one she actually had.

Mike and Miranda had made their announcement shortly after she and Travis had arrived at the gathering. Miranda was pregnant. And, to Shana's bewilderment, after doing her very best to look properly surprised and awed, everyone else in the room hooted and laughed as if all this was already old news to them.

Tugging on Travis's arm, she drew him aside when she'd gotten his attention and whispered in his ear. "I thought we were supposed to be surprised."

The feel of her warm breath along his skin generated a shiver that slid up and down his spine. Travis paused half a second to savor the sensation before he banked it down and pretended to be unaffected.

"Right now, you're still the outsider. You weren't supposed to have a clue. I forgot to tell you about the one-upmanship that runs rampant through my family." He laughed, shaking his head. "Even if they hadn't expected her pregnancy to be what the big announcement was all about, this crew would have acted like they had."

"And you?" Shana challenged. "Did you actually know, or did you just guess?"

"Well," he hedged, "I guessed. But then, I'm usually right when I guess," he added quickly. "Besides, Mike knew I guessed so there really wasn't all that much sense to pretend otherwise."

Shana thought about having the thunder of an exciting announcement like a pregnancy stolen away from her. For a second, she felt sorry for Miranda. "Not even for Miranda's sake?" she pressed.

"Miranda understands," he told her. "She's one of us now," he said, as if that explained everything.

There was a warmth in his voice when he spoke of his sister-in-law. Shana caught herself being envious of Miranda.

All traces of envy vanished in under an hour because, within that space of time, Shana found herself being effortlessly absorbed into the Marlowe family network. She almost didn't realize what was happening, but suddenly, there was no "them" and "her," there was just one large homogenous group that incorporated all of them. She loved it.

She was comfortable with them almost from the moment she crossed the threshold. And the favor was returned.

The Marlowes were a family that her father would have easily fit into. He was the one with the knack of making people feel at ease and at home.

It would be nice to have him on the receiving end for a change.

To her everlasting sorrow, the party started breaking up. When she glanced at her wristwatch she saw that somehow, magically, the evening had slipped away and it was now a few minutes after ten. Everyone there had work the next day, or, in Kelsey's case, school. It was time to get going.

She never felt so reluctant to leave in her life. Especially after each person in Travis's family hugged her goodbye. It made her feel as if she'd known them all forever.

"Thank you for having me," Shana told Kate sincerely as she and Travis finally made their way to the front door.

"Thank you for coming," Kate countered, brushing a quick kiss against her cheek. And then she took both of Shana's hands in her own. "Maybe next time, you'll bring your father along."

Caught off guard, Shana looked at Kate in surprise, then slanted a glance in Travis's direction. She didn't recall mentioning her father during the evening.

"I told her about your dad and his restaurant," Travis explained.

"He and Trevor can put their heads together and compare recipes," Kate told her with a soft laugh. "Might be good for both of them."

"Among her other wonderful attributes, my wife is a frustrated social director," Bryan told Shana as he joined them at the front door. He slipped his arm around Kate's waist and gave her an affectionate squeeze.

"And where would you all be if I wasn't?" Kate asked, a hint of the Irish lilt she'd toned down over the years making a brief appearance.

"Lost, my love," Bryan freely admitted with sincerity, pressing a kiss to her temple. "Utterly lost. No question about it."

"Hey, you two, get a room," Kelsey called out from the foot of the stairs.

"They did," Trevor shot back. "And you're the unfortunate result."

He ducked as his sister sent a coaster flying in his direction.

"Okay," Travis announced, "Now it's really time to go." Kissing Kate goodbye, he threaded his fingers through Shana's and crossed the threshold, leading her down the driveway.

Shana turned and waved at the couple in the doorway before quickly falling into step beside Travis, who still held her hand captive.

"They look cute together," she told him. "Your parents," she added when she realized that everyone in the room had been paired off except for Kelsey. "You can just see how much they love each other."

It was something he'd come to take for granted over the years and he stopped now to reflect on Shana's comment. "Yeah, you can," he agreed.

Reaching his car, Travis took out his keys and pressed the security release. It beeped at him in response. Leaning over, he opened the door on the passenger side for Shana and held it for her as she got in.

In this age of independence, Shana wasn't accustomed to acts of polite chivalry. But she certainly could get used to it. Suppressing a grin, she got into the car.

After depositing her purse on the floor, she reached for her seat belt and fastened it in place.

"You know, they're the kind of parents I used to fantasize I had. Young, loving." She saw the quizzical look enter his eyes. "Oh, don't get me wrong," she was quick to tell him, "my parents were great and I loved them dearly. Nobody had a better pair. It's just that, when I was in elementary school, whenever anyone saw either one of them at school events, or coming to the school yard to pick me up, they always thought they were my grandparents until I corrected them."

"And that embarrassed you," he guessed.

"And that embarrassed me," she repeated. Shana flushed slightly as he pulled away from the curb. "I really didn't have much backbone when I was that age," she confessed.

He saw it slightly differently. "Kids that age just want to fit in," he told her kindly. "Anything that might make them stand out feels awkward. You just wanted to have parents that blended in with everyone else's."

The soft laugh was self-deprecating. "That's pretty intuitive of you."

"When your stepmother and one of your brothers are both child psychologists, you tend to pick a few things up here and there," he said casually.

She liked that. Travis didn't put on airs, didn't act as if he felt that he was something special, even if he was. And that made him even more special in her eyes.

"What else did you pick up from your stepmother and Trent?" she asked.

He thought for a moment as he made a right turn at the end of the block. "That raising kids is hard. But then, I knew that firsthand." He made his way to the left turn lane at the next light. The streets were relatively empty. "There were times I was pretty sure my father was going to have a nervous breakdown. My brothers and I kept wiping out nannies and he didn't have the time to handle us himself. Nor do I think he could have done it emotionally, at least, not at the time. He was dealing with his own sorrow over losing my mother," he explained. Travis slowed down as amber turned to red at the cross section. "It's to his credit that he didn't just farm us out to some unsuspecting relative on the eastern side of the continent."

"Did that cure you of wanting kids?" It was an exceedingly personal question, one she wouldn't have ordinarily asked, but she found herself wanting to know more about him. To know a host of things about a man she professed no attachments to.

"Of wanting them?" he asked, then shook his head.

"No. But of having them? Well, first I'd have to find someone who was willing to go in on the deal with me." And someone he'd be willing to share more than just his roof with, he added silently. "That's the hard part."

"You make it sound like a brokerage deal instead of a marriage."

He thought of the couples he knew outside his family. And he'd discovered years after his mother had died, that even his parents seemed to be on their way to a divorce. That was why his mother had been on that plane without them, going on a solo vacation to rethink what she actually wanted—and didn't want—from life.

"These days," he told Shana, "it winds up being that more often than not."

She looked at him for a long moment, not altogether certain which side of the fence she wanted him on. "Don't believe in marriage?"

The shrug was casual. Travis saw no point in mentioning his parents, especially in light of how happy his father was with Kate.

"With all three of my brothers married—and happy—it's a little hard *not* to believe in the institution, but I do know that maintaining a marriage is a lot of damn hard work."

"Anything that's worth having and keeping usually is."

They were silent for a few minutes. He slanted a glance at her as he took another right turn.

"How do you feel about marriage?" he heard himself asking.

"I don't feel anything at all about it." After breaking

up with Kevin, she deliberately banked down all her emotions, refusing to revisit a place where she'd been vulnerable. "I'm too busy to give it the time it deserves," she continued evasively.

That was called learning from her mistakes, she added silently. Because when she was engaged to Kevin, she thought about little else. Until Kevin shattered the dream—and along with it, her.

Travis pulled up to the Tudor-style house in the middle of the block. The house that she now shared with her father. He turned off the ignition, but rather than open the door and get out, he faced her, mildly amused and more than a little intrigued.

Moonlight became her. Shimmering along her skin, it made her look like an earthbound goddess.

What did a goddess's kiss taste like?

The thought seemed to materialize out of nowhere, but it caught his attention and he turned it over in his mind. Slowly.

"Let's see," he said, his eyes skimming along the contours of her face, "we've discussed kids and marriage, all before we've even kissed." Was it his imagination, or did his throat tighten just a wee bit as he made his observation?

All the butterflies in Shana's stomach flared to life but she summoned her courage. "There's an easy solution for that," she told him, then congratulated herself that her voice didn't crack or tremble.

He raised an eyebrow. "Oh?"

"Yes, 'oh.'"

And then, before she lost her nerve, Shana leaned over into his space. Framing his face with her long, delicate fingers, she pressed her lips against his. The moment she did, something happened. Every fiber of her being came to life.

She froze in place even as she felt things inside her heating. Shana's heart rate accelerated as Travis deepened the kiss. Control slipped away from her. She'd started this, but he was definitely finishing it. And, quite possibly, her.

Just like that, she went from being the initiator, the leader, to the follower. There was no strength within her to resist, no strength to keep from melting almost completely.

She belonged to the moment.

To him.

He tasted of something dark and compelling. She wanted more.

A small moan escaped her lips as she continued to slant them over his. Things went on inside of her that she hadn't expected to feel ever again. Had specifically forbidden herself ever to feel again.

Yet here she was, feeling. Being a pawn in a game she no longer controlled.

Fun, remember? You're just having fun, nothing else. Because if it was something beyond that, something more, she didn't know what would be left this time when it ended. Because, inevitably, it would end. No man could understand that her father, the man to whom she owed so much, had to come first right now. The male ego wouldn't allow that.

Despite the mental pep talk, Shana felt her heart racing in her chest by the time Travis drew his lips away. Trying to collect herself, she watched a smile curve the corners of his mouth.

"Well, now that we've gotten that out of the way," he quipped, letting his voice trail off. His eyes looked deeply into hers. There was mischief in them, he thought. She caught his soul at that moment.

Only one way could she regain control here, and that was to initiate action. "Wait," she murmured seductively, "I don't think it's quite out of the way yet," she told him.

"Whatever you say," he murmured, taking her back into his arms.

The second time around was even better than the first. His head began to spin as if he'd had consumed his alcohol too quickly. She tasted of all things sweet and intoxicating. Travis struggled not to push it further, the way everything within him begged him. It felt as if every nerve ending he possessed had gone on high alert.

He took a long breath, released it slowly, as if steadying himself. And then he smiled. "I'd better get you home," he told her. He didn't know how much longer he could trust himself.

"Yours?" she asked, her voice low, like amber liquid sliding along the sides of a brandy glass.

The sound of her voice made his very skin tingle. Damn, but she had some effect on him. This was decidedly a first.

"That is up to you," he told her evenly, his voice a low rumble, his eyes pinning her in place.

She'd expected something else. To be coerced, convinced. Swept away. Disappointment whispered through her system. "You don't care one way or another?"

"Oh, I care," he assured her. "I care very much. And it's definitely 'one way,' and not 'the other.' But the choice isn't mine," he pointed out gently. "It belongs to you."

Was he being chivalrous, or thinking ahead to avoid the blame when this turned sour? "You don't want any responsibility in this?"

He started to wonder about the men who had been in her life. Had they scarred her? Made her distrust her feelings? Not lived up to her expectations?

And how would she feel if she knew that he was privy to a secret that would set her life on its ear? A secret he wasn't free to share with her, even though he encouraged the man she thought was her father to tell her?

He pushed those thoughts to the side, focusing only on the moment. The breathtaking, soul-stirring moment.

"I don't want you to feel pressured or rushed," he confided.

She took a deep breath, like someone who was about to plunge off a high cliff. "So this would be my decision entirely?"

He crossed his fingers mentally, afraid to breathe. "Yes."

She raised her eyes to his, stirring something deep in his gut. "And if I asked for your input?"

God, but she was driving him crazy. It was all he could do not to pull her into his arms, not to kiss her over and over again until there was no room for thought, only action.

But he, like his brothers, had been raised to afford women the utmost amount of respect, to put the woman's needs and wishes high above his own.

Still, he owed her the truth if that was what she was asking for. "Oh, lady," he whispered, gently brushing a curl from her temple, "I think you know what my input would be."

She leaned closer to him again and he thought she was going to brush her lips against his one more time. Instead, she whispered, "Tell me."

The soft stir of her breath seduced him, creating havoc.

"I want to take you home and make love with you all night long, or until we're both too exhausted to breathe, whichever comes first."

She took a deep breath and for a moment, he thought that common sense would prevail. She was going to tell him that he should just drop her off here.

But she surprised him by saying, "Take me to your apartment."

His heart pounded in his ears. "You're sure?"

She pressed her lips together, her eyes watching his lips. She forced herself to think of nothing but this moment. And the ones that were to hopefully follow this night. "I'm sure."

Travis didn't remember turning the ignition back on, didn't remember driving the car to his place.

But he must have because, somehow, they got there. In record time.

Chapter 10

It was all that Shana could do to keep her hand still. She was trembling inside when Travis opened the passenger door for her and helped her out of his car.

Her fingers were icy.

Travis looked into Shana's eyes. There were things going on that he couldn't quite get a handle on.

She was afraid, he realized.

Of him?

That was absurd. No one was afraid of him. He didn't have that dangerous edge that he sometimes found himself envying when he saw it in other men.

Was she afraid of herself?

That probably made more sense. He knew firsthand that it could be unsettling to discover yourself a prisoner of desires and emotions. Right now, he was experiencing a little of that himself.

He wanted her. Very, very much. But as much as he did, he didn't want fear to be part of the equation.

His hand tightened on hers and he gave it a warm, assuring squeeze. When she raised her eyes to his quizzically, he said, "Maybe I'd better take you back home."

Shana's eyes widened with confusion. "Why?"

He smiled and gently touched her face. This was costing him. A lot. But she had to be here for the right reasons. "Because you have the same look in your eyes as a kid who's about to be inoculated—trying to be brave but pretty much scared out of their mind."

Shana squared her shoulders and lifted her chin. "I'm not afraid," she protested, her voice still breathless.

The expression on his face told her he didn't believe her. "Then why do you sound as if you can't catch your breath?" he asked.

Was he really this noble? If so, that made him one in a million. For just a moment, she rethought her newly adopted "no strings" policy. No, it was better that way. Removed so that even though passion could find her, pain couldn't.

"Maybe it's because you've stolen it away," she finally said.

He was about to say something about being very flattered, but the words never reached his lips. She reached them first, pressing her soft mouth against his.

The woman packed quite a wallop. Her kiss seemed to channel all of the wild, unnamed feelings that could rise up between a man and a woman, swirling around like the beginnings of a tornado funnel.

Her breath might not have been stolen away, but damn, his certainly was. Right along with everything else that ordinarily made him a clear-thinking, logical man. In less time than it took for him to blink, Travis found himself reduced to a mass of desires and passions, of wants and needs.

Heat began to radiate from him, mingling with hers until it all but threatened a meltdown, right here, standing beneath his covered parking space. For all the world to witness.

Someone driving by honked their horn, presumably at them.

With almost superhuman effort, Travis forced himself to draw back, even though all he wanted to do was continue on this path. He wasn't about to put on a show for the immediate public like some hormonal adolescent—even though that was exactly the way he felt right now.

"I guess maybe you don't want to go home," he said softly, trying to catch not just his breath but his mind, which had fogged up like a medicine cabinet mirror during a prolonged shower.

She could feel her heart slamming against her rib cage. *More,* an inner voice begged. *More.*

"No," she whispered, "I don't."

His smile burrowed its way under her skin, creating havoc. Where was even a shred of control? she wondered. What was happening here?

"Then I suggest we get out of the parking lot before I lose the ability to resist you," he told her.

Shana felt her mouth curving. He made it sound as if she was the one in control of the situation. They both knew she wasn't. At this point, she had no idea who, or even what, was in control.

Pressing her lips together, she nodded. The inside of her mouth felt incredibly dry as she murmured "Okay."

The apartment complex was composed of two- and three-storied buildings, all less than two years old. There was a freshness about them, even at night. Travis's apartment was on the ground floor, less than thirty feet away from the covered parking space where they were standing.

It felt more like fifty miles.

During the walk to his apartment, he found he needed time to pull himself together, as he silently marveled at how quickly this statuesque woman with the radiant smile could disarm him. How quickly she'd reduced him down to his most primal level.

Unlocking the door, Travis reached inside and turned on the light for her as she entered.

There were newspapers, a few of the standard magazines devoted to the state of the economy, and folders scattered about both on his small kitchen table and the slightly scarred dark marble coffee table in his living room.

He thought about straightening the piles, then decided it was too late for that. "I wasn't expecting company," he confessed, closing the door again.

Trying to regain use of her knees again, Shana looked around. His apartment had just the right amount of clutter, she caught herself thinking. Judging by its state, there hadn't been a woman here for a while. The thought pleased her.

As did the realization that he hadn't planned on seducing her when he picked her up tonight. If he had, his apartment would have been neater. First impressions and all that.

The smile on her lips seemed to come of its own accord.

This was all spontaneous. Which was the way she wanted it. Spontaneous meant being free. Meant that there were no ties, which was, she kept silently insisting, the way she wanted it. If there were no expectations, there could be no sense of disappointment, no hurt feelings or the sharp, stabbing sensation of being let down in the future. No having your heart trampled by someone you trusted to put your feelings above his own—or at the very least, on an equal footing.

Shana turned toward him. He was watching her reaction, she realized. Her smile deepened. "It's a nice apartment."

As if coming to, Travis cleared away a stack of folders that had been on the sofa, placing them next to other piles on the coffee table.

Nodding toward the sofa, he asked, "Would you like to sit down?"

I'd like you to kiss me. Now. Before I lose my nerve. Before I can think this through to the end and run out the door.

Rather than say anything, Shana moved her head from side to side, her eyes never leaving his face.

Travis felt his pulse speed up. When she didn't say anything further, he went with his instincts, foregoing the role of the host and banking down the sense of uneasiness that wove through him. Uneasiness over the fact something more was going on than he was currently aware of.

As a rule, Travis didn't believe in casual sex without some kind of feelings involved. And with feelings came the need to have everything honest and above board.

But this time, the uneasiness came because he wasn't being honest. He was privy to a secret. A secret he was bound by law and, more importantly, by ethics to keep from her. It wasn't his secret to tell.

But it was hers to know and if, no, *when,* she realized that he knew and had kept it from her, their connection would be forever tarnished.

He knew in his pounding heart that he should call a halt to this. That it wasn't right, in a strange way, taking advantage of her. But damn, when she looked at him like that, with her mouth so close to his and her body so warm and willing, it was hard to focus on doing the right thing.

All he could think of was making love with her. Slowly and with feeling. For hours on end. He felt the need down to the very bone.

"Shana," he began, not really knowing a single word of what he was going to say after that.

Which made no difference because he never got to say more.

The look in her eyes pulled him in. Something inside of her seemed to be calling out to him.

And then he was kissing her.

Kissing her as if his very soul hung in the balance.

From the moment he surrendered to the feeling that had all but a stranglehold on him, Travis knew he was hers. Hers the way he'd vowed to be for a very long time, if not forever. He wasn't a strong believer in the "many-fish-in-the-sea" philosophy. That reduced women—and love—to the point where one was practically inter-changeable for another, one was as good as another. He had never believed that.

Instead, he'd believed that finding the right woman was a very difficult task and even when you thought you'd succeeded, most likely you hadn't.

But it was getting harder for him to think, hard to do anything but go with these sensations that were all but burnt into him. The more he kissed her, the more he wanted to kiss her. The more he touched her, his hands brushing against her face, her throat, her shoulders, the more he absolutely *needed* to touch her. It was either that, or cease to be.

Shana's breath kept hitching in her throat, becoming almost a solid entity and impossible to purge from her lungs. It happened each time she felt Travis's hands pass over her body.

He touched her almost reverently, as if she would break at any moment. Her flesh all but burned as her desire to have his hands pass over it increased. Shana desperately wanted him to touch her without fabric getting in the way.

She arched into his fingers, into his palms, even as her mouth was sealed to his.

With her blood surging in her veins, her hands began quick work of yanking his jacket from his arms, feeding it to the floor. No sooner was that barrier out of the way than she began tugging at his shirt, fumbling at the buttons, desperately pushing the material from his shoulders.

Her fingers touched strong, rigid muscles along his arms. The hardness she discovered excited her, fueling the fire that had sprung up in her chest. In the very center of her core. A shiver danced down her spine even before she felt him remove her blouse. His movements were as slow and deliberate as hers had been fast and erratic.

Shana froze, absorbing every touch, every brush of his fingertips.

There was no way for her to bite back the moan that escaped from her lips as his hands cupped her bare breasts.

It was just the beginning.

Breathing hard, she threw back her head. His lips trailed along her throat, creating a new wealth of sensations within her that peaked and spiraled as they drew her further into a hot, burning ecstasy that winked in and out of her body.

Clothes continued raining down, hers mingling with his in a silent, impromptu game of strip poker where the stakes were higher than just money.

And once there wasn't a stitch of material left between the two of them, their limbs tangled as closely as their lips did.

Travis kissed her over and over again, grazing every

part of her body, destroying all sense of time and space and launching her into a nether world of glorious sensations.

It was only through supreme effort that she managed to hold on to her being enough to return the favor, pulling him into the same vortex. Every pass of his hand drew one from her in kind.

Her fingers feathered along his heated skin, forcing him to rein in what he so badly wanted to explode. But Travis refused to place his own pleasure above hers, couldn't allow himself to reach or indulge in that ultimate of sensations before he knew that she was there, as well. More than that, he wanted her to sample its fruits and pleasures before his own became a reality.

Gently pushing Shana back onto the sofa, he proceeded to pleasure them both by feasting on her body. His lips, teeth and tongue tantalized and teased her, each working their magic as they reduced her to a mass of moist, palpitating, wanting flesh.

Shana suddenly arched and cried out his name when the first crescendo grabbed her up, holding her a prisoner in its grasp.

Stunned, awed, she wasn't completely certain what it was that he had done, only that she'd never felt something of that magnitude before. Moreover, she was almost desperate to feel it again.

Sweet exhaustion wrapped itself around her even as she arched against his mouth, silently supplicating for one more sample, one more explosion to cherish before she woke up from the dream.

As she arched, she could feel Travis's lips form a smile against her stomach. Before she could ask if he was laughing at her, the question faded from her brain. Because she felt him begin to slowly, then swiftly fulfill her unspoken request. Felt the nerve endings within her scrambling for higher ground as his tongue dipped further into her, teasing the most tender of areas, making it come alive with sensations.

The second climax came more swiftly than the first, knowing which trail to follow. Everything within her quickened.

Her heart pounding wildly, Shana tried to focus as Travis slid his slick body over hers, all parts touching, branding her.

She felt exquisitely alive from the tips of her hair to the bottom of her toes.

His face level with hers, she still could only see him through a cloudy haze. And then his hands were laced through hers even as he raised himself up for leverage.

The next moment, he was joining his body to hers. They fit like two halves of a whole, coming together for the first time since the dawn of creation. And then, his eyes on hers, Travis began to rhythmically move.

Shana matched him, her own desire getting the better of her. She thought her heart would explode in her chest as they went faster, scaling the high plateau. And then, a moan echoed in her throat and she just barely managed to keep it from surfacing. Arching her body so hard, she thought she had sealed herself to him, her backbone fusing with his.

They were one.

Just as powerfully as it had begun, the sensation began to recede.

The inferno became a manageable fire and the pounding of her heart softened into a quiet, fading drum roll.

He rolled off her and for a long moment that seemed almost endless, there was nothing but silence and the sound of their labored breathing.

Because she couldn't steady it, Shana began to think her breath would never become manageable again. But then it did, ushering in reality. And with it an odd sadness that it was over.

And she wanted more.

Shana pressed her lips together and forced herself to turn her face toward his.

"Just what did your mother put into that cake?" she asked.

He was busy watching the way her chest rose and fell with each breath. And how each breath she took made him want her again that much more. When he heard her voice, he roused himself, trying to focus on what she was saying. He failed.

"Excuse me?"

She lifted one indifferent shoulder and let it fall again, doing her best to seem nonchalant.

"Poor attempt at humor," Shana confessed. And then she added, because even though she silently insisted that there were to be no strings, no relationship in the offing, she still found that she needed him to know this about her. "I've never gone to bed with someone I hardly knew before."

His eyes dipped to the cushion she was lying on and he smiled. "Well, technically, we haven't gone to bed yet."

Was he playing with words? Why didn't he feel as disoriented, as dazed and as wondrous as she did? Exasperation rang in her voice as she corrected, "Okay, I've never gone to sofa with a man I hardly know."

Travis raised himself up on his elbow to see her expression. As he spoke, he trailed his fingertips along her skin, skimming the area between her breasts. He watched her flesh quiver slightly. The sight excited him all over again.

"Is that a compliment?" he asked.

She hadn't meant it to be, at least, not consciously. But now that he asked, who knew? Certainly no other man had ever made her want to become this wanton creature she'd just glimpsed, even if she was cocooning herself in excuses.

"That's a confession," she finally answered.

"Confessions are for the guilty," he told her softly. He caressed her face, exciting them both. "Don't feel guilty, Shana."

I feel guilty enough for both of us, he added silently before he succeeded in blocking out his thoughts again.

"There's nothing to feel guilty about," he assured her.

"I don't feel guilty," she protested and then realized that, oddly enough, she didn't, even though she'd expected to. With effort, she tried to keep the mood light. "I just don't want you thinking that I do this with every man who takes me to a family celebration."

Leaning over her, his hand resting on the hollow of her waist, he lightly brushed his lips over hers. "I don't," he assured her.

She caught her breath. There went her heart again, beating out a drum solo that throbbed its rhythm through all her pulse points. "No strings," she managed to say to him.

Travis wasn't thinking about the existence of strings. He was thinking about losing himself in her all over again.

"No strings," he echoed, not even sure what he was saying. All he knew was that he wanted her just as fiercely as he had the first time. With a wild desire that shook him to the very foundation of his being.

Chapter 11

"Anything wrong?" Bryan put the question to his son almost two months later after silently debating whether or not to intrude.

It was approximately an hour before regular office hours and Bryan had come in to look over a brief. Expecting to be the only one in the office at this time, he was surprised to see Travis's door open and more surprised to see Travis. Curious, he approached the office and found his son sitting at his desk. But rather than working, Travis appeared to be staring off into space, a pensive frown on his lips.

Travis seemed oblivious to his surroundings until Bryan asked the question. When his son raised his eyes to look at him, Bryan thought Travis seemed troubled.

If something was bothering him, why hadn't his son come to him?

When Travis made no reply, Bryan prodded a little. "Anything I can help with?"

Travis blinked, and gave a slight shake of his head, not in response to the question, but as if to shake off the mood he'd sank into. "Excuse me?"

Bryan took that as an unspoken invitation and crossed the threshold. He also closed the door behind him, just in case Travis needed to share something in confidence.

"I'm not nearly as good as Kate is at this," Bryan began, picking his way carefully through the conversation, "but I have noticed that you've been a lot quieter lately than normal. Your workload hasn't changed, so I'm thinking that maybe something else is going on."

Bryan paused, waiting. Knowing how, when he was Travis's age, or actually, up to and including the point when he had first met Kate, he'd hated anyone poking around in his life. Feelings had always been private and off-limits as far as he'd been concerned. It took Kate to teach him otherwise. She'd taught him that to be part of a family, to love and be loved, meant that you shared not just the good times but the pain as well.

"Is it that girl you brought to the house for Mike and Miranda's party?" Bryan guessed.

"Shana."

"Shana," Bryan repeated, nodding his head. "Is it her?"

By nature, Travis wasn't defensive, but he felt himself becoming just that. "Why would you ask me that, Dad?"

The very question—as well as Travis's tone—told Bryan that he'd guessed right.

"Because, for most of your life, you haven't exactly been auditioning for the part of Casanova. You're more private than your brothers. We didn't even meet Adrianne until you were briefly engaged to her. So naturally, when you brought Shana to the house, we thought..." Bryan stopped his line of thought and shifted gears. He was relatively new at this. Kate handled all the heavy-duty emotional stuff. But Kate wasn't here right now, so he did the best he could. "Anything wrong between the two of you?"

"Wrong?" Travis echoed.

It was a blatant stall tactic as Travis tried to frame his thoughts. The answer was yes—and no. No because for the last two months, they'd seen each other almost every evening, if for only a little while. And most evenings turned into a perfect slice of heaven that found them in each other's arms, making love or just simply enjoying the moment with one another.

Perfect, except for the hot bullet of guilt that kept digging its way further into his gut.

Shawn hadn't told Shana, the way he'd initially suggested, that she was his granddaughter and not his daughter. Hadn't prepared her for the shock that lay in wait for her. It seemed somehow inevitable to him that Shana would eventually find out, one way or another, that Susan was her mother, not her sister. The truth always had a way of surfacing, usually at the most inconvenient time—and sooner rather than later.

He'd prodded Shawn once more, but then Shana had entered the room and any conversation on the topic was suspended.

Permanently, if he was any judge of the situation.

Compounding the problem, even though Shawn refused to stay away from his beloved restaurant, the man seemed to be growing paler, his gait heavier, his breathing more audible and even labored at times. Travis couldn't divorce himself from the uneasy feeling that time was running out. For all of them, not just for Shawn O'Reilly.

Sitting there beneath his father's scrutiny, Travis blew out a breath. He needed help. Advice. At the very least, he needed to have a lifeline of some sort thrown to him. Because as it stood now, he couldn't seem to navigate these waters on his own.

Taking another breath, Travis dove in. "Dad, did you ever break a confidence?"

Bryan slowly crossed over to the desk now and took a seat in front of it.

"Professionally or privately?" He studied Travis's face as he asked his question.

"Both," Travis responded, then gave a vague shrug of his shoulders. This was definitely complicated. "I guess professionally to start with."

"No, but I've been tempted more than once," Bryan confessed honestly. "Ultimately, you have to do what *you* feel is morally right. Clients trust us to keep their secrets. If that trust is gone, sacrificed for whatever reason, we'll only get half the picture from them. It ties our hands and keeps us from rendering the proper kind of service to our clients."

"What if keeping that confidence is morally wrong?" Travis pressed.

"By whose judgment?" Bryan paused, waiting. When Travis didn't answer immediately, Bryan took the logical guess, "Yours?"

"Yes." But this wasn't just an arbitrary feeling. "There's more to it than that."

Bryan gave him the rules that had always guided his judgment. "We're custodians for these people who come through our office doors. We give them the benefit of our experience and we advise them. But ultimately, all decisions whether or not to share with the world—or their families—what they have told us in confidence belong to them. We can't presume to usurp their authority. We certainly can't force our sense of values on them if they don't want them."

But those were lofty platitudes. Travis, he could see, was obviously in anguish. Though he wasn't nearly as expressive or sensitive in dealing with his children as his wife was, it still bothered him to see one of his own suffering like this.

Getting up, he put his hand on Travis's shoulder. "You want to talk about it?"

If only he could. But that wasn't allowed, even between colleagues of the same firm. He adhered to strict observance of the privilege. Travis shook his head. "You know I can't."

"Hypothetically, then," Bryan suggested.

Travis eyed him quizzically.

"I can take a few educated, general guesses," Bryan explained, "and you can indicate to me if I'm on the right trail." He didn't wait for an answer. Instead, he began theorizing out loud. "You have a piece of information that you feel will have a large impact on someone's life if they were privy to it." It didn't take too much of a stretch to assume that this had to do with Shana.

"I think I'd use the word *devastating*," Travis told him.

Bryan nodded as he took in the information. "Seeing as you're not given to exaggeration, this—whatever it is—must be pretty bad. Because if it was good, then keeping it a secret from that person wouldn't make you chafe against your oath." Travis merely nodded in response. The rest was easy, at least in theory, Bryan thought. "And you're afraid, if she finds out and then learns that you knew this all along and kept it from her, it might cause a rift between the two of you."

A *rift*. What a nice, civilized word for the tearing apart of something unique and precious. Because, despite her protests to the contrary, despite her monologue about "no strings," he'd become fairly confident that they had something special between them. And that she was falling in love with him—as much as he with her.

Travis laughed softly under his breath as he looked at his father. "I guess you're the one who's given to understatement in the family."

Bryan watched him for a long moment. "Just how important is this girl to you?"

"I don't know," Travis answered too quickly. Self-preservation had him making the vague denial. But he needed to be honest here. Honest with his father as well as with himself. And the truth of it was, Shana mattered more to him than any other woman ever had.

"Very."

He raised his eyes to his father's, waiting for a reaction. Hoping for perhaps a dispensation from the man who'd taught him everything he knew.

His father's answer surprised him.

Kate was right, Bryan thought. This *was* serious. All four of his boys, gone down like dominoes. At least he still had his daughter. Kelsey, bless her, was as serious about men as a comedy routine.

"If she is that important to you and she's worthy of those feelings, then she should understand that you're not able to violate the oath you took before God and the state of California. Your integrity is at stake. Not to mention that people go to prison to protect the attorney-client privilege. If it's important enough to stand up to higher authority in order to protect it, she should be able to understand that it has nothing to do with her and everything to do with integrity and the law."

Travis laughed shortly as he shook his head. He would have thought his father would have understood the position he found himself in. After all, his father had Kate to set him straight.

"Dad, women are built different than men," Travis pointed out tactfully. "And, even though intelligence is found on both sides of the gender gap, they do think differently than we do."

But some things, Bryan liked to think, were universal. "Not if she loves you. That is what we're talking about, right? Love."

Travis proceeded warily. He would hate to be wrong about Shana and then have it come back to bite him. It was better if he left her side of it vague. "Yes. On my side. I don't know what it's like for her. She keeps talking about 'no strings.'"

Bryan smiled. Again, he had his answer. "I had the same conversation, years ago, except that was my mantra. Trust me, if 'no strings' crops up more than once in the conversation—even the sum total of conversations—the lady doth protest too much."

Travis was about to agree but just then, the intercom on his phone buzzed.

When he picked the receiver up, Bea crisply informed him that "Ms. O'Reilly is on line two for you. She sounds really upset."

He told her, Travis immediately thought, feeling both relieved and anxious at the same time. Does she know I knew?

He looked up at his father. "I've got to take this, Dad." The rest was left unsaid as his finger hovered over the lit button beneath line two.

Bryan was already on his feet. He only paused to say, "I'm around if you need to talk more," before he crossed to the door.

Travis waited until his father closed the door and then got on. "Hello?"

"Travis, it's Dad."

He could tell by the tone of her voice it had nothing to do with a confession and everything to do with Shawn's health. Travis was on his feet, ready to take off. "Where are you?"

"The house. I'm waiting for the paramedics. Travis, he's barely conscious—" Her voice cracked and he heard a sob.

"I'll be right there," he promised. "Just hang on."

"Hurry," Shana implored before breaking the connection.

Travis was out the door in less than a heartbeat.

"Bea, call my appointments for today and reschedule all of them, please," he instructed as he passed her desk.

"What'll I tell them?" she called after him, rising in her chair.

"That there's been an emergency," was all he said before disappearing around the corner.

Travis didn't remember the drive. He hardly remembered getting into his car. The squeal of tires against asphalt echoed in his ears as he pealed out of his parking space and onto the street. The road was a blur of lights and he was vaguely conscious of eking through half a dozen yellow ones.

He reached Shana's house in record time.

The ambulance, its rear doors hanging open, dominated the driveway. Travis pulled up to the curb just as the front door to the house opened. Two burly paramedics were propelling a gurney between them, and Shawn O'Reilly was strapped to it. Shana hurried along one side of it, holding on to Shawn's hand and talking to him.

Shawn wasn't responding. As Travis got closer, he saw that the man was unconscious.

The sight of her grief-stricken face tore at his heart. "Shana?"

She turned then, using the wrist of her free hand to brush aside the tears that had stained both of her cheeks. She almost sobbed when she saw him. "Oh God, Travis, I'm so scared."

Very gently, the paramedic closest to her separated her hand from her father's in order to load the gurney into the ambulance.

Travis immediately put his arms around her, wishing he could protect her from the pain he knew had to be ripping her apart.

"It's going to be okay," he promised, knowing that he had no right. But all he could think of was that he wanted to give her something to cling to, something that would kindle hope in her heart, no matter how irrational such a promise might be.

The paramedic in charge turned to look at Shana after he and his partner had loaded Shawn and his gurney into the ambulance. His chiseled features softened in the face of her distress.

"You can ride with your father if you like," he offered kindly.

A ragged breath escaped her lips. "Travis?"

He wasn't sure if she was asking him what to do, or if she wanted him to come with her.

"Go ahead," Travis urged, nodding toward the ambulance. "I'll be right behind you in the car," he said.

Like someone lost within the sticky webbing of a deep trance, Shana barely nodded in acknowledgment of his words. Waiting for the gurney to be secured into place, she then scrambled behind it, not waiting for anyone to help her get inside.

She looked lost as the doors closed on her, Travis thought.

He turned to the second paramedic who had secured the rear doors. "How is he?"

The attendant looked as if he debated answering, then finally shook his head.

"It doesn't look good, but you never know," was all he said before hurrying off to the front of the ambulance and getting in behind the steering wheel.

Travis ran to the curb and got into his car. The moment the ambulance left the driveway, he was right behind it.

The whirling lights and high-pitched wail of the siren parted the traffic before them. Travis remained directly behind them the entire way to Blair Memorial Hospital.

Mentally, he kept his fingers crossed, hoping that no police vehicles were in the immediate vicinity. Because of the speed he was maintaining, he knew he'd be pulled over and precious time would be wasted as he explained why to some officer of the law. Time that would be inadvertently taken away from Shana.

He didn't want her arriving at the hospital without him, didn't want her facing the possible death of a father by herself.

It turned out that luck was with him. Travis managed to reach the hospital less than two heartbeats behind the ambulance. Rather than find parking on his own, he pulled up to the valet booth and surrendered his keys to the parking attendant beside the hospital's E.R. entrance. He all but tossed the keys to the tall, thin, blondhaired man as he hurried to where the ambulance had parked.

"Name?" the attendant called out after him.

"Marlowe. Travis Marlowe. With an *E*," Travis shouted back. He never even turned around or broke stride.

Travis reached the ambulance just as the rear doors opened again. He was there in time to help Shana get down after the gurney was unloaded. There in time to see her eyes red and swollen from crying.

Instantly the worst occurred to him.

Still holding Shana's hand, Travis looked toward the first paramedic, a silent question in his eyes. The attendant's expression was troubled, but he and his partner were still continuing to work over the unconscious patient.

It was Shana who filled him in. "His heart stopped." She stifled the sob that had almost escaped. "On the way over, his heart just stopped." Again she paused, letting out a shaky breath as she fought to regain control over her emotions. "But the paramedic managed to get it started again."

Her lower lip trembled. Shana caught it between her teeth, stilling it. Trying desperately to pull herself together. If she came apart, she couldn't do her father any good and he needed her right now. More than ever. Questions about his condition needed to be answered, medical history had to be given and she was the only one who knew the names of the doctors, the different medications. The only one who knew the various and sundry incidents that had brought her father here this morning.

How was she going to be strong when all she wanted to do was cry? To shout and demand to know what he thought he was doing to her. He wasn't supposed to die. Not yet, not today. Not now.

Not ever.

She wasn't ready to be alone. To be an adult and not anyone's daughter. She *needed* her father to go on living.

I didn't mean it, all those times I thought you were too old. I never *meant it. You're not too old, you're younger than I am. In your heart. That same heart that's giving you so much trouble now.*

Taking a deep breath, Shana squared her shoulders. They were going to get through this, she and her father. There was no other alternative.

When she felt Travis's arm go around her shoulders, she blinked.

"I'm all right," she told him, her voice distant.

Breaking free, she followed Shawn's gurney as the paramedics pushed it through the automatic rear doors of Blair Memorial's Emergency Room.

Chapter 12

They lost no time closing ranks around Shana, gathering as if she were one of their own.

Travis couldn't remember *ever* being more grateful for his family. All it had taken for this to come about was telling Kate what had happened. She'd called him on his cell phone less than an hour after he'd arrived in the emergency room. That made it fifty minutes after Shawn O'Reilly had died without regaining consciousness.

When he'd heard his stepmother's concerned voice on the phone, asking how Shawn was faring, it wasn't difficult for him to figure out the chain of occurrence. Bea had probably mentioned to his father that he'd flown out of the office like a bat out of hell after getting the call from Shana. His father, putting two and two together, had called Kate, and Kate, ever intuitive, had called him.

But it didn't end there, with an expression of concern followed by the request that he convey her condolences to Shana. Less than twenty minutes after terminating her phone call to him, Kate arrived at Blair Memorial. Reasoning, undoubtedly, that Shana needed the comfort of a mother, Kate silently took the grieving young woman into her arms.

Startled, Shana resisted for perhaps an emotion-filled moment—if that long—then dissolved into tears and melted into Kate's arms.

Travis heard Kate murmuring soft endearments, most in English, a few in the dialect from the old country from which she originally hailed. All meant to soothe and give comfort.

After several minutes, Shana drew back, trying to pull herself together. She was behaving like a child. And she was no longer anyone's child, she thought sadly.

"You must think of me as an idiot." Her cheeks tear-stained and flushed with embarrassment, Shana's words were addressed to both Kate and Travis.

"I think of you as someone who's grieving," Travis told her. Since Kate was here with her, he felt he could leave her alone for a few minutes. "I'm going to go see about the arrangements," he said to Kate.

Shana had drawn away from Kate and was now standing by Shawn's gurney. There hadn't even been time to transfer him to one of the E.R. beds. The moment his gurney had been pushed through the elec-

tronic doors, his heart had stopped again. E.R. physi-
cians had quickly converged around Shawn, exercising
desperate life-saving measures that ultimately failed.

All but two nurses had retreated from the area after
time of death had been called. The nurses now looked
to Travis before taking care of the deceased's body.

Travis glanced at Shana's face. She was completely
focused on Shawn. "I think she still needs a little more
time," he told the older of the two women.

The nurse nodded. "Tell the poor dear to take all the
time she needs." Pausing for a moment, she lowered her
voice as she asked, "Do you know what funeral parlor
she wants to use?"

When he had dictated the terms of his will, Shawn
had also been very thorough about his final arrangements. He'd left nothing to chance, choosing the casket
he wanted and where to hold the service. He'd paid for
everything ahead of time—something that he'd instinctively known was in short supply. The man had left a
copy of all the instructions with him. Travis now nodded
in response to the nurse's question.

As he gave the woman the name of the funeral parlor,
he heard Shana's whisper-soft voice behind him as she
said her last good-bye to the only father she'd ever
known.

Travis turned around to see Shana holding Shawn's
hand in hers. "I forgive you, Daddy. I forgive you for
leaving me. But it's going to be a sad, lonely world
without you in it."

Leaning over the man's lifeless body, Shana pressed

a kiss to his cheek, struggling to keep from shedding fresh tears. But one lone tear gave her away, sliding down her cheek onto his.

Travis came up behind her, gently taking hold of Shana's shoulders and turning her around to face him. Stifling a sob, she buried her face in his chest and remained there, lost in silence, trying to make sense of the large, cold new world she suddenly found herself in.

"You're coming home with me tonight," he told her. "I won't let you be alone."

Shana began to protest, but her heart just wasn't in it. She didn't want to be alone in the house she'd shared with her parents, not just yet. The silence would be unbearable.

"You're both coming home with me," Kate informed them. Travis looked at her in surprise. He opened his mouth, but Kate was quick to silence any protest. "I'm not taking no for an answer, so you might as well just save your breath. Both of you." She took Shana's chin in her hand and lifted up the young woman's head until their eyes met. "Travis can tell you that once I make up my mind, there is no changing it."

"It's true," he told Shana. "Dad calls her the most stubborn woman on the face of the earth, or did," he amended, remembering what his father had said about his sister, "until Kelsey started talking back."

Shana knew they both meant well and she tried hard to smile at them in response, but the ache inside of her chest and stomach had formed a huge, huge bottomless hole and she felt as if she was free-falling.

So she merely nodded and let herself be led off. Later

she'd be the strong-willed woman her father had raised her to be. But right now, she was just his little girl, grieving because he was forever lost to her.

Shana came for the night.

She stayed for the week.

Every time she would say something about going back to her own house, someone—Travis, Kate, Bryan, Kelsey, even his brothers and their wives—would come up with a reason why she needed to remain where she was. With them. His brothers and their wives no longer lived there, but they all seemed to make a point of dropping by, just to talk, to hang out for an hour or so, asking her how she was doing and if there was anything she needed. They all stood by her throughout the soul-wrenching ordeal of the wake.

She'd never met a family like the Marlowes. They made her feel as if she was one of them. As if she mattered to them. It helped to gradually make the pain manageable.

Shana kept the restaurant closed that week, although Kate, Travis and even Trevor and his wife, who had their own restaurant to run, offered to help keep Shawn's Li'l Bit of Heaven open for her.

The wake—Travis mercifully handled all the details—ran the traditional three days and every evening it was standing room only in the viewing room. Shana was touched to see just how many people had loved her father. But even with all these people who came up to her, offering their condolences, sharing stories about her father, she was acutely conscious of the one person who continued to be missing.

On the third day, as the end of the viewing time approached, Shana watched the door intently, hoping against hope to see the person who counted most. Travis could sense the tension searing through her. Coming up behind her, he gave her shoulder a quick, gentle squeeze, silently assuring Shana that he was there for her.

"She's not coming," Shana said more to herself than to him. Turning around, she looked up at Travis. "I had every newspaper in the state run the obituary so Susan could see it no matter where she was staying. I know she must have seen it," she insisted, for once not bothering to bank down her anger. "How could she not come?"

He didn't want to sound as if he was defending Susan. He just wanted to soothe her anguish. "From what you told me, they didn't leave things in a very good place. Maybe now she's feeling guilty that she didn't try to mend those fences before he died. That would make it hard for her to come see him like this."

"Maybe," she murmured. "But she could still come," Shana insisted. "Still pay her respects. He *was* her father."

"Guilt makes people act in odd ways," he told her, thinking of his own guilt and how heavy it was becoming. He fervently wished that Shawn hadn't shared his secret with him. Or that the man had told Shana before he died. "Maybe she's afraid that you'll hate her."

Shana shook her head. She wasn't like that. "I don't hate her. I hate the way she behaved," she explained, "but I don't hate Susan."

Travis slipped his arm around her and gave her the

only bit of hope he could. "Maybe she'll come to the funeral tomorrow."

"Maybe," Shana echoed.

She didn't.

Although there were throngs of people at the service and later at the cemetery's grave site, and even though Shana gratefully found herself protectively cocooned by Travis and his family, her periodic search of the one familiar face she needed to see yielded no satisfaction.

Susan didn't come.

"Maybe she missed the obituary," Travis suggested as they rode back from the cemetery in the limousine. "People don't usually read the obituaries until they think they're old enough to be in one."

"Maybe you're right," Shana agreed hoarsely. There was no point in driving herself crazy. But she did need to let Susan know that their father was gone. "God, I wish I knew where to find her."

Maybe it was better this way, Travis thought. At least, for the time being, it pushed the confrontation he sensed would come to the fore. From the little that Shawn had told him, he definitely didn't get a good feeling about the woman.

Shana eased the front door closed behind her, then turned on the foyer light even though it was only early afternoon.

The silence that emanated from all four corners was incredibly deafening. She kept expecting the sound of her father's laughter or his footfall on the marble floor.

There was nothing.

Opening the restaurant for business again yesterday had been difficult enough. But there'd been enough noise there to fill all the empty spaces. To keep her from thinking.

But coming here, knowing she would never hear his voice again, never see him sitting before the television set, laughing at some inane sitcom, was almost too much for her. She came perilously close to falling apart.

She was deeply grateful that Travis refused to let her do this alone even though she'd insisted she was up to this. Secretly, in her heart, she knew she wasn't. It bothered her that she wasn't stronger, that she didn't live up to her own self-image.

But Travis and his family, bless 'em, had all but pooh-poohed that away.

"Strength only comes after vulnerability's been conquered—which means you had to be vulnerable first in order to be strong," Travis told her authoritatively, doing what he could to soothe her unrest. "And there's no way in hell—or heaven—that I'm letting you walk into that big old house for the first time since Shawn died by yourself."

So far, she hadn't had to. He'd purposely sent his sister to collect whatever clothes and other items she'd needed for her stay at his parents' house. He wanted to spare her as much pain as possible, until the inevitable came to light.

She turned toward him now and put her arms around his neck. There was a look in her eyes he couldn't quite read. Apprehension slipped in, even as he tried to block it. "You know, I really don't know what I would have done without you this last week."

He brushed aside a strand of hair that fell into her eyes, thinking how strange fate was and how much she'd come to mean to him. If Shawn hadn't come into his office to put his affairs in order, he would have never known someone like Shana existed.

And, by the same token, he wouldn't be carrying around the burden of a secret that could very well pull them apart.

"You would have gotten through it," he assured her with conviction. "I have no doubts that you would." God, but he loved her. He couldn't imagine going back to a life without her. "But I am glad I could be there to make all this just the tiniest bit easier for you."

"More than a tiny bit," she told him.

There was still this hollow, burning sensation in her chest, but because of Travis, she knew it wouldn't undo her, wouldn't unravel her. Knew, too, that someday, it would get easier.

She was nobody's little girl anymore and that realization was really painful. But Travis was with her and he meant the world to her.

"He liked you, you know. My dad," she added in case Travis wasn't following her rambling speech. "He really liked you a lot."

She smiled, thinking of the less-than-subtle hints her father had dropped. Her father thought Travis was perfect for her. She rarely knew her father to have been wrong.

"I think he was hoping that he'd found someone for me—" Belatedly, she realized what that had to sound like to Travis. She didn't want him thinking she was envisioning wedding invitations dancing in her head. "—Not that I'm saying—"

He didn't want her spoiling the moment with a declaration of a non-relationship, even though he had a feeling it would be a protest without any true feeling behind it.

"Shh," Travis chided softly, putting a finger to her lips to silence her. He loved watching the way her eyes widened. "You might not be," he told her, "but I will be. Once everything's in order, I think I'd like to talk about the future," he told her. He felt his way around slowly, never taking his eyes off her face. Watching it for a reaction. "Our future," he specified, silently holding his breath.

She heard the blood rushing in her ears. "Together?"

The wonder in her eyes almost made him laugh. He had a feeling that wouldn't have gone over too well. She was being vulnerable. Well, hell, he couldn't remember when he'd been more vulnerable himself. "That's the gist of it."

She didn't want to misunderstand or take something for granted. She needed to have everything spelled out. "How together?"

Was she backing away, or testing the waters? He wasn't sure. But there was only one way to find out. He had to dive in first.

"As together as two people can be," he told her. "You know, rings, church, wedding dress." He thought of his family. They could come on strong at times. "In-laws who don't really understand the meaning of the words 'not butting in—'"

"Don't make fun of your family," she protested with feeling. "I love them." She took a deep breath. "And I love you." Another deep breath followed before she could continue. "So, if you're asking me to marry you—"

"Maybe I just like wedding dresses," Travis teased, trying to keep a straight face but without a whole lot of success.

She laughed before completing her sentence. "—if you *are* asking me to marry you, the answer's yes. Oh, yes," she repeated with enthusiasm, rising up on her toes as she tightened her arms around his neck.

He tucked her even closer against him, reveling in the feel of her body pressed so close against his. "So we can have strings?" he asked innocently, referring to her ever-present "no strings" mantra.

She felt suddenly so giddy, her head was beginning to spin. *Oh, Daddy, I wish you could have been here. I wish you could have heard him.* And then it occurred to her, given the faith that had been instilled in her as a child, that her father could very well be privy to all this right now.

The thought made her smile—and gave her peace.

"We can have a whole string factory," she told him with a laugh. Shana tightened her arms around his neck and kissed him as hard as she could, giving him her heart as well as her pledge.

Lost in the depths of the kiss, Travis didn't realize what he was feeling at first. Dampness. His cheek was wet.

Shana was crying.

Drawing back, he saw the telltale evidence on her lashes. "Oh, please don't cry," he implored. "I don't know what to do when a woman cries."

A woman's tears always made him feel so helpless. He could handle almost anything else but that. And why did women cry when they were happy?

He was assuming she was happy, he thought in minor desperation.

She had a ready solution to the dilemma for Travis. "Just kiss me," she instructed, offering up her mouth to his.

His smile was wide, filtering into his eyes and down into his soul. "I can do that."

Travis lowered his mouth to hers and kissed her with every fiber of his being. She'd said yes!

Lost in the moment and the promise of the life that was to come, a life that would find them forever joined, neither one of them heard the door being unlocked.

It wasn't until the door was firmly closed again—slammed really—that either one of them realized there was someone else in the house with them.

Shana's heart hammered hard as she pulled her head back and looked toward the foyer.

For just a split second, she thought it was her father walking in.

Her head knew that wasn't possible, but her heart was having trouble catching up.

But it wasn't her father in the foyer.

"Well, I must say that your taste in men has improved," the woman standing there said. "By about a hundredfold."

There was blatant approval in the deep brown eyes as they swept rather possessively over Travis, taking inventory of all his parts as if they were hers for the taking. She was accustomed to being the pretty one, the one who drew all the attention when she entered a room. Shana had always been the afterthought.

But these days, her lifestyle had left its mark on her and that mark was less than kind. She seemed worn around the edges, like a woman who knew her time was limited and was desperate to hang on to the trappings of years that had already passed by.

The smile on the woman's lips was almost predatory as she extended her hand, her scarlet nails curving like talons. "Hello, I'm—"

"Susan," Shana said in a hoarse, stunned whisper.

Chapter 13

"Hello 'little sister,'" Susan said mockingly.

The tall, almost too-slender woman looked around the foyer as if to reorient herself. Or maybe Susan tried to imagine the house without their father, the way Shana had been doing just moments ago.

Susan tossed her dark brown, blond-streaked hair over her shoulder and haughtily lifted her chin. There was more than a hint of a smile on her lips. "So, he's really gone, huh?"

Shana felt her back going up at the irreverence in Susan's voice. She tried to tell herself it was because Susan was hurt that she would now never get a chance to work things out with their father. There would be no truce in the offing, no coming to an understanding. Just a permanent wound and a scab running over it. That had to be painful.

She took a breath before answering. "Yes, he's really gone."

Susan made a disparaging noise as she shook her head. An enigmatic smile creased her lips. "Bet that came as a shock to him. Dad always seemed pretty confident he was going to live forever."

She'd been gone all this time and now that she was here, Susan was being sarcastic and disrespectful. Shana took offense in her father's name.

"He was sick for quite some time, Susan. Which you would have known if you ever bothered to come around."

"Yeah, well, whatever," Susan shrugged her slender shoulders dismissively. "That's all in the past now, isn't it? The important thing is, did I miss the reading of the will?"

Shana's eyes blazed. Was that all their father was to her? An inheritance? "You missed the funeral, Susan," she retorted, struggling to keep her resentment from pouring out.

Whenever she became angry at the way Susan neglected him, her father would say that Susan had a lot to deal with and that they should cut her some slack. Even so, she knew that her sister's behavior, her absence from his life except on those occasions when she needed money, hurt him deeply. And that was something she was having trouble forgiving right now.

"Yes, but did I miss the reading of the will?" Susan repeated with feeling, making it clear that all she cared about was what was coming to her, nothing more.

How could this woman be Shana's mother, Travis wondered silently. "Not yet," he informed the older woman.

Susan looked at him with renewed interest. "Did he cut you in?" she asked, mildly curious. "Is that how you know?"

"I was your father's lawyer," he told the older woman evenly. "He had me place all his accounts, the restaurant and the house in a living trust."

"Doing the two-step with the tax man, good for him." Susan nodded her approval of the news. "He always was a sharp old guy, at least when it came to managing his money." She flashed an inviting smile at Travis. "So what's say we cozy up a little and get that pesky will reading over with?" And then she added a coda to her suggestion. "Unless it's all just divided up between Shana and me. In that case, just get me my half of everything and I'll be out of your hair." Her words were addressed to Travis, but she was looking at Shana as she said them.

Shana began to set the other woman straight, but Travis shook his head, stopping her. This was his job, and he took over.

"It's not divided up that way," he told Susan evenly.

Suspicion entered the dark blue eyes and her expression hardened. "Oh? And just how is it divided up?"

Travis took out his card and offered it to Susan. "Why don't you come by my office and I'll go over it with you then?"

She pushed aside his hand, disregarding the card.

Her eyes narrowed as she looked at him. "Why don't we just go over it now?" she countered coldly.

"He doesn't have the will with him, Susan," Shana said.

The smile was malevolent. "No, but I've got a feeling lawyer-boy here has it memorized." She cocked her head, eyeing him as she came closer. "Don't you, lawyer-boy? You and Shana cook up a little something between the two of you?" she prodded. "Get my dad to sign a new will? Maybe hold his feeble hand to get the signature right?" she suggested, anger evident in her expression.

"Don't be ridiculous," Shana snapped, defending not just her father, but Travis as well. "Nobody made Dad do anything. It was his idea." Her anger rose. "Maybe if you had shown up a few times over the last few years, you would have seen for yourself that he was clear-headed until the end."

Susan was not buying it. "But you whispered in his ear, didn't you, Shana?" the older woman accused sarcastically. "Talked about how awful I was for not being around, playing nursemaid like you. Being a saint always became you."

Shana bristled at the suggestion that she had turned her father against Susan. If anything her father tried to get her to forgive Susan. "I never talked against you."

"Yeah, right," Susan snorted. "Pure little Shana, never did anything wrong in her life." She looked at Travis haughtily and with pity. "Pretty boring, isn't she?"

He found his hold on his temper slipping through

his fingers. "Why don't you stop right here, Ms. O'Reilly?" he said coolly. "Before you say something you might regret."

Susan laughed. "I *never* regret anything I say, lawyer-boy." The smile vanished as quickly as it had materialized. Anger took over. "Now, just how unequal is this damn will?" she demanded.

Shana put out her hand, asking Travis to keep silent. This was for her to say. "Dad left everything but one bank account to me, but—"

What she was going to say was that, despite Susan's treatment of their father, she wanted the division to be more equitable than that. But it was just going to take her some time to raise the money in order to pay her sister more. Shana never got the chance. Susan cut her off with a ripe curse.

"The hell he did," Susan spat. Her face contorted with barely suppressed rage. "Dad wouldn't do that to me."

No, not if you'd showed just a little compassion, a little affection. Something. But you didn't. "You hurt him a lot, Susan."

She blew out a breath and bit off another oath. "Lucky for him he's not here right now because I'd show him just what real hurt is." Susan tossed her head, sending her hair flying over her shoulder. "He can't do that. I'll take this into court, Shana," she shouted indignantly. "I'm his only daughter. I should get everything. He can't just do this to me," she insisted furiously.

Travis felt his stomach tighten into what amounted to a clenched fist.

Confusion etched into Shana's features. For a second, she stopped breathing. "What are you talking about?" she demanded.

Susan turned on her. "What are you, deaf now, too, as well as conniving?" And then she stopped abruptly, staring at the confused expression on Shana's face. The truth came to her riding on a lightning bolt. And then she laughed. It was a harsh sound. "Oh, this is rich. Really rich." Her face invaded Shana's space. "You don't know, do you?"

Here it came, Travis thought, desperate for a diversion. He caught hold of Susan's arm, pulling her away from Shana.

"This isn't the time or the place," he told Susan angrily. "If you want to go over things, you and I can go to my office—"

This time it was Shana who waved him into silence when he made the suggestion, her eyes pinned on the sister she had once idolized. "What are you talking about, Susan? *What* don't I know?"

Susan looked like she was almost enjoying this, revealing the secret she'd once insisted be kept. "That I'm his only kid. His only daughter."

Shana didn't understand. What was Susan talking about? Was she just playing with her head?

"Then what am I?" Shana demanded hotly, her mind refusing to give any credence to anything that Susan was saying. On more than one occasion, Susan had been caught in a lie. She could lie so smoothly, so effortlessly, that she probably believed what she was saying.

Instead of answering, Susan laughed. "Oh, this really is rich," she repeated. She was enjoying prolonging this. "He never told you, did he? That old man actually kept his word. Who would have thought it?" she marveled. "He promised he wouldn't tell, you know." Her eyes slid over toward Travis. "But he told you, didn't he, lawyer-boy? A man confesses things to his lawyer he wouldn't share with his own family."

There was an unnamed panic festering and growing in the pit of her stomach, making her ill. Shana looked from Susan to Travis.

Was that guilt she saw? Why? Did he know what her sister was talking about? If he did, then why hadn't he said anything? If it concerned her, she had a right to know. Why would he have kept it from her?

"What is she talking about, Travis?" she asked, her throat aching.

"Yeah, 'Travis,'" Susan mimicked in a sing-song voice, "tell Little Miss Priss what it is that I'm talking about."

She didn't have time for games. Not wanting to wait, Shana took a stab at it, coming up with the only thing that would make sense under these circumstances. "Am I adopted, is that it?"

Entertained, and feeding on Shana's distress, Susan laughed again. "Girl gets a gold star—for guessing half right. You're adopted all right, Shana," she confirmed wickedly, her voice throbbing with glee.

Why wouldn't Dad have told her she was adopted? There was no shame in that, in being selected rather than conceived. "But that still makes me his daughter."

The smile on Susan's lips grew even more malevolent. "It gets a little more complicated than you think, 'little sister.'"

"Is this another one of your games, Susan?" Shana shook her head. "It's not going to work. You can't rattle me the way you could Dad. I'm not as forgiving as he was."

"Oh, I bet I can," Susan countered sweetly. "I bet I can *really* rattle you, Shana." Again, she drew closer until she was all but in Shana's face. "You weren't Shawn and Grace's daughter," she informed her haughtily. "You're *my* daughter."

Standing beside her, Travis felt Shana start to sink as her knees buckled. And then she galvanized, squaring her shoulders and holding her head up high. "You're lying."

Placing a hand to her chest, Susan embodied the very portrait of innocence. "Now why would I lie about something like that?"

"Because you always lie, Susan. Every time Dad cornered you and you had your back to the wall, you lied."

A smug expression on her face, Susan shifted her eyes over to look at Travis. "I'm not lying now, am I, lawyer-boy? You know that, right?"

A second set of eyes, fear and apprehension rising in them, turned toward him.

"Is she, Travis?"

Tired of the game, Susan waved at Travis, silencing anything he might have to say. "If you don't believe me, check your birth certificate."

Her birth certificate. Of course, why hadn't she thought of that earlier? A thread of peace wove through her. Susan was just trying to agitate her. "I've seen my birth certificate, and it has Shawn and Grace O'Reilly down as my parents."

Susan laughed harshly at Shana's naiveté. "Not that one, you idiot. That's the one that Dad had doctored in case you ever wanted to see it. The real one's in his safety deposit box at the bank. Don't hold it against him," she added magnanimously. "I was the one who made him do it. Actually, it was Mom and me. It was the only way I'd agree to having you."

Traces of resentment filled Susan's voice as she continued the narrative that was shattering Shana's world.

"Dad wanted you to know the truth, but I figured having a kid was going to be too much of a drain on me. Besides, the kind of life I was leading wouldn't be any good for a kid. Dad certainly told me that enough times." Anger filled her eyes. "Mom wanted to raise you so I said, 'Go ahead.' And just to keep things from being complicated, I told her she could pretend to be your mother." Susan shrugged as if the story was boring her even as she related it. "They got another chance to be parents and maybe do it right this time and I got a chance to be free." She tossed her head triumphantly. "A win-win situation all around."

Shana's heart beat so hard, she didn't understand how it wasn't breaking through her rib cage. "I don't believe you."

Another vague movement of Susan's shoulders told Shana what the woman thought of her protest. "Believe what you want. But I'd check that safety deposit box if I were you." And then a malicious smile curved her lips. "So, 'daughter,' I guess I'll see you in court." When Shana stared at her, stunned, Susan mocked her. "There's no way in hell that you're going to get what legally belongs to me."

Travis was still holding his business card in his hand. Turning around to face him, Susan plucked the card from his fingers, tucking it into the bosom of her blouse. With a smug, superior expression, she patted it into place.

"You'll be hearing from me, lawyer-boy," she promised. Turning on her heel, Susan walked out of the house. Nothing but the sound of her high heels clicking across the marble disturbed the silence.

Shana stood there for a long moment after the front door closed. She was numb.

Concerned, Travis tried to bring her around. He put his arm around her. "Shana—"

It was as if suddenly a switch had been thrown and she came to life. Shana shrugged away his arm, but her eyes remained unfathomable as she raised them to his face.

"Is it true?" she demanded. "What Susan just said, is it true? Did my father—did Shawn—" Damn, she didn't even know what to call him. If he wasn't her father, then he was her grandfather, but she was having a hard time thinking of him that way, reconciling what she'd just learned with what she'd always believed. "Did he tell you that Susan was my mother?"

It was here. The moment he'd been instinctively dreading ever since Shawn had confided in him. *Damn it, old man, why didn't you listen to me and tell her right away?*

Where did he start? How did he make amends and still have her understand why he'd done what he had? Again, he tried to draw her into his arms.

"Shana—"

Shaken, feeling betrayed and more abandoned than she'd ever thought possible, Shana took a step back, keeping out of his reach.

"Answer me," she ordered, struggling to keep her voice from cracking. "Did he tell you that Susan was my mother?"

If he said "yes," would she let him explain? One look at her face told him the answer to that. But still he tried to calm her. "Shana—"

There was an apology in his voice.

And then she knew.

Shana sucked in her breath. It felt as if she'd just been shot. She could have cried.

"He told you. It's true. Susan is my mother." She shut her eyes. The pain only increased. "Oh God." Opening them again, she saw that he was about to enfold her in his arms. She couldn't bear to have him touch her. He'd lied to her. By not saying anything, he'd lied to her. "Why didn't you tell me?" she cried angrily. "Don't you think I had a right to know?"

"It wasn't my secret to tell," he answered simply, praying she'd understand. "Shawn was my client. Anything that he said to me in confidence had to remain that way."

She heard only one thing. "So you were loyal to him, but not me."

She was intelligent. She had to see the difference. "It's not like that, Shana."

It was *exactly* like that, she thought angrily. Her eyes narrowed to slits.

"Oh?" she retorted. "Then what is it like?" She didn't wait for him to answer, even if he could. "You were sleeping with me, Travis. For God's sake, you just proposed to me," she shouted at him. "I thought that meant you cared about me."

That had nothing to do with his duty, didn't she see that? For the first time since he'd made up his mind what he wanted to do with his life, he hated being a lawyer. "I did. I do—"

"If you cared so much, why didn't you tell?" she asked. "Why didn't you warn me instead of letting me be hit right between the eyes? People who love each other look out for one another. They protect each other. They don't let them walk through a minefield without at least giving them some kind of a warning."

If he could have played this out differently, he would have. He would have sold his soul to keep her from hurting like this. But all he could say in his defense was the truth. "Ethically, my hands were tied."

"Ethically?" Shana echoed in disbelief. "What about morally? What about me?" she demanded. Didn't he care that her whole world had just been destroyed? That the very foundations had been shattered into little tiny pieces? "Did you laugh to yourself every time you heard me call him 'Dad'?"

"It wasn't like that and you know it," he insisted.

"The moment he told me, I advised your father—your grandfather," he amended, "to tell you." He could see she didn't believe him. "But he was afraid to. He'd promised his wife that he would never say anything to you about it, but that doesn't mean that his conscience didn't bother him. It did. He told me it did. And the longer he kept it from you, the more afraid he became that if the truth finally did come out, you wouldn't forgive him for deceiving you."

Travis's words did nothing to abate her anger. "That was his excuse, what was yours?" she asked.

Now that he was living this dreaded moment, it was worse than he'd anticipated. He tried again to reason with her, to make her understand that he was shackled by the very rules he'd sworn to uphold.

"Shana, I was his lawyer."

"And you were my lover," she countered. And the latter was supposed to trump the former. "But I guess I see where your loyalty lies." She took a breath. Her heart ached beyond belief. "No wonder no one likes lawyers."

He didn't care about anyone else, he cared about her. "Shana—"

She didn't want to hear it. Didn't want to hear excuses. Didn't want to hear his voice. "Please leave," she requested, her voice cold, distant.

Travis was prepared to dig in. He needed to fix this before the damage hardened. "I don't think you should be alone at a time like this."

The flat of her hand against his chest, she caught him by surprise as she pushed him back. "I don't care what you think. Just go." She looked at him, and she almost caved, but then she dug deep for resolve. "Now."

She was too angry, too hurt, to be reasoned with, Travis thought. He had no choice but to go. "All right," he agreed.

Travis left the house feeling worse than he could ever remember feeling.

Chapter 14

Shana hardly slept that night.

Tossing and turning, she couldn't find a place for herself, not in any position. She felt as if she was the victim of a one-two punch aimed straight to her gut. Her stomach physically ached and she felt lost, disoriented. Sick. She had no idea what to feel, what to think.

It was awful enough to have lost her father once. But twice? Once to death and once to reality since he wasn't really her father at all, but her grandfather. For the life of her, she couldn't really say which left her more devastated.

She'd grown up trusting him with her whole heart and soul. She would have bet her very life that he'd never lied to her.

How *could* he have lied to her like that all these years? How could he not tell her that he was her grandfather instead of her father? She wouldn't have loved him any the less for it. She wouldn't have cared what he called himself. What she cared about was that he'd lied to her—and kept on lying, day in, day out.

Could he have loved her at all and lied like that?

And her mother, her mother was really her grandmother. What was she supposed to make of that?

Up was down, black was white and nothing, nothing made sense anymore.

Everything she thought she knew was a lie. The carefully crafted world she'd embraced was cracking apart on her, built on a foundation that didn't exist, on a tissue of deceptions that broke apart and dissolved like snowflakes on the water.

Who *was* she?

Her mother, her *real* mother, hated her. She could see it in Susan's eyes. Damn, how could she think of her as anything else but Susan after all this time? Susan, the sister who never had any time for her.

And then there was the biggest mystery of all. Her father. Her real father. Who was he? Did Susan even know? Was *she* ever going to find out?

Did it even matter anymore?

She was numb.

Shana sat up in bed, hugging her knees to her chest. Too shell-shocked to even cry. Why hadn't someone told her? Why hadn't someone cared enough about her to tell her the truth? Or was she so insignificant to these people she'd spent her whole life loving that a lie served as much purpose as the truth?

Travis.

God, she'd actually thought she loved Travis. And that he loved her. What an idiot she was.

Why hadn't Travis told her the truth when he found out? Why had he gone along with this lie? Didn't she matter enough even to *him* to deserve the truth? How could he align himself against her like that?

Exhausted, Shana fell back against her bed. Grabbing her pillow, she hugged it to her and suddenly the floodgates opened and the tears came again.

She sobbed her heart out, feeling more alone than she ever had before in her life.

She cried for a very long time, long after dusk, and then twilight crept into the room, followed by a moonless emptiness. Too exhausted to get up to turn on the light, she let the darkness blanket her. Praying for oblivion, Shana finally fell into a dreamless, restless sleep.

Morning found her no better. She stumbled through a routine that had long been ingrained in her, going through the required motions to make herself presentable to the world. Showering, brushing her teeth, getting dressed.

And somewhere in that time, she made up her mind what she needed to do.

Within an hour, she was behind the wheel of her vehicle, driving to the suite of offices where her late father's—no, her late grandfather's lawyer, she amended, was located.

God, but that was going to take forever to get used to, she thought gloomily. Even though she'd grown up thinking that the couple who raised her were old enough to be her grandparents instead of her parents, she'd come to accept their age as a badge of courage. She thought of them as two people who had ventured into territory normally reserved for the much younger, because God had blessed them with a child.

Except that it wasn't God, but Susan who'd "blessed" them, she thought darkly. Susan, who changed men as often as some people changed coffee filters.

As she drove, moving in and out of traffic she hardly saw, Shana tried to remember if there ever had been even a single instance where Susan had behaved motherly.

None came to mind.

Instead, she remembered the snide remarks, the put-downs. But kind words? Those were so scarce, they were close to nonexistent. Mostly, if she and Susan interacted at all, she came away feeling that she was in the older woman's way. An annoyance Susan had just as soon ignore than speak to.

Now she realized just how much of a hindrance she'd actually been.

Tears started to form again and she silently upbraided herself. You'd think she would be completely out of tears after last night. She wasn't going to cry about this, she ordered herself fiercely. Crying wouldn't change anything. She just needed to adjust and move on. There were no other options.

Because she had always been so organized, practically from birth, appreciating order and always striving to tie up loose ends, Shana thought it was only fair for her to inform Bryan why his firm's services would no longer be needed. She realized that she should actually be telling Travis, but she just couldn't make herself face him. It would be like ripping open her wound all over again. His part in this hurt her most of all. Because his loyalty should have been to her and it wasn't.

Which meant he really didn't love her, no matter what he said yesterday, and she had just been fooling herself all along.

A lot of that going on lately, Shana mocked herself, her hands all but maintaining a death grip on the steering wheel as she drove.

Those strings she'd initially denounced were strangling her. That's what she got for allowing herself to get tangled up in them.

Bryan was on his feet, swiftly crossing to his door the moment he'd been informed by the head receptionist that Shana was here to see him.

"Hold any calls," he told the young woman at the central desk as he ushered Shana into his office. "I don't want any interruptions," he added firmly, in case there was any doubt in the matter.

A soft sigh escaped Shana's lips as the door closed behind her. She deliberately locked her knees in place and remained where she was, afraid to take a step. Afraid of faltering if she did.

"I take it Travis told you."

"Not in so many words, but I know that there's some kind of problem that's come up."

Travis had been more closemouthed than ever when he'd seen him this morning, only mentioning that there might be a lawsuit over O'Reilly's will in the offing.

Bryan looked at the young woman who had managed to capture his son's heart and saw the troubled expression in her eyes.

"Judging by your face, it's a big problem," Bryan surmised. "Bigger than the suit."

Tired and preoccupied with the upheaval in her life, Bryan's words initially didn't make sense to her. "Suit?"

"The lawsuit." When she still continued to eye him blankly, he elaborated. "Your sister is contesting your father's will. She says he wasn't of sound mind and was coerced into practically cutting her out."

"Oh, that." Shana moved her shoulders in a vague shrug.

That was the least of it, she thought. It wasn't even part of the big picture that tortured her.

And then suddenly, she played back Bryan's words in her head. He'd referred to Susan as her sister and Shawn as her father. She was so accustomed to those labels that she hadn't realized the man was wrong.

Which meant that he didn't know.

Hadn't Travis told him? "My father?" she echoed, looking at Bryan uncertainly.

He saw no reason for her confusion. "Yes."

Her eyes narrowed as she studied Bryan's face. Was

he being polite? Lying? She was no longer a good judge of that. "Then you don't know?"

"Know what?" he asked quietly.

"That Shawn O'Reilly wasn't my father, he was my grandfather. And Susan is my mother." Bryan seemed genuinely surprised by this revelation. "So, Travis didn't tell you?"

"No," he answered, thinking that the news explained a lot—about a great many things. "And he wouldn't have been able to if this was something that Shawn had told him in confidence." For a moment, he stopped being a lawyer and switched to being a father. "I take it that this is the 'something' that has you so upset?"

He was being kind. She didn't want kind. Kind undid her, creeping through all the barriers she'd set up and tearing them apart.

"Wouldn't you be in my place?"

"Probably." He could see that his admission surprised her. It was hard maintaining distance from a woman who reminded him of his daughter. "Here, why don't you sit down?" Taking her arm, he gently led her to the sofa that was against the far wall.

Shana sat down on the edge of the cushion, as if bracing herself to spring up at any moment. Bryan sensed the aura of tension around her. "I came to tell you that I wouldn't be needing your firm's services any longer."

"I think you might," he contradicted. For now, he attempted to appeal to her logical side. "Given the lawsuit."

Shana waved the words away. "I don't care about the

lawsuit, Mr. Marlowe. Susan—my mother—whoever she is," she said in mounting frustration, "she can have it all."

"I don't think that's what your father—your grandfather," Bryan softly corrected himself, hoping that her emotional turmoil wouldn't cause her to do something rash, "would have wanted. Otherwise, he would have specified it in his will. I think he felt that of the two of you, you were the one most qualified to carry on where he left off. You were the one who appreciated the sacrifices that he'd made to build up the restaurant. He probably felt that Susan would sell it the first chance she got," he said pointedly, "and then squander the money. Judging from past experiences that seemed to be her usual way of operating."

Shana's jaw hardened. She knew it. "So Travis did tell you."

Bryan shook his head. "Only what was common knowledge." He looked at her closely, remembering how distressed Travis had seemed the other week, wrestling with the dilemma. "If Mr. O'Reilly told him something in strictest confidence," Bryan repeated pointedly, "Travis was ethically bound to keep it that way. Private. Breaking that oath for any reason without leave to do so could have gotten him disbarred. Your grandfather trusted him."

Bryan saw tears shimmering in her eyes as she looked at him defiantly. "And what about my trust?" she asked. "Didn't that count?"

"It counts," Bryan allowed. "But it should only be shaken if you discovered that Travis *didn't* keep his

vow not to repeat what was told to him in confidence."
He got down to the crux of that matter that he sensed
she, in her hurt state, was missing. "Because once a man
breaks his word, then how do you know if you can trust
him the next time? There's always that nagging doubt
that he'll break it again."

Shana laughed shortly. "Forgive me, Mr. Marlowe,
but that's lawyer double-talk."

"Is it?" Bryan challenged, his voice low and all the
more powerful. "Think about it, Shana. Change the
sequence around for a moment," he suggested. "Just
for now, put yourself in your grandfather's place with
this big secret to protect. What if it was *you* with a
secret and you, for whatever reason, had confided it to
your lawyer. To Travis," he added for emphasis, underscoring his son's professional capacity. "A secret that,
once known, would have an effect on your grandfather's life. An effect you might be afraid of it having.
How would you have felt if Travis, once he was ap-
prised of this secret, had turned around and told your
grandfather?"

Shana pressed her lips together. "You're twisting it."

Bryan took her hands, creating a bond that tran-
scended his professional standing. This, he sensed,
could be his future daughter-in-law, if only he could
break through her hurt.

"No," he told her, "I'm only reversing positions." He
paused, then added, "Would it help you to know that
Travis told me the other week that he was having one
terrible moral dilemma honoring his ethical principles?"

Startled, she looked at him in surprise. "He told you that?"

Bryan nodded. "He laid it out hypothetically and didn't go into any specific details, but I knew Travis was privy to something that was killing him not to reveal." His smile was encouraging. "I'm guessing that this was the secret."

Maybe yes, maybe no. She really didn't have the strength to debate that right now.

Since Travis's father was being so honest with her, she laid out the confusion she was experiencing. Maybe, by saying something, she could feel better about the situation.

She raised her eyes to his. "Do you know what it's like to find out that everything you've ever believed was a lie?"

"I don't," Bryan admitted. "But I do know what it's like to discover that something I believed to be true wasn't."

He was thinking of his first marriage. A marriage he'd believed to be happy, only to discover that his late wife felt herself trapped not just by him, but by their four sons. When she'd finally admitted her feelings to him, told him that she needed to leave, perhaps permanently, he'd felt as if his world had completely caved in on him.

He could only guess that Shana was going through something similar.

Bryan offered her the same kind of hope that Kate had given him when she came into his life. Love went a long way to helping someone heal.

"Travis isn't very vocal about his feelings. But I can tell that he cares for you a great deal, Shana. If he didn't tell you it was because he couldn't, not because you didn't mean enough to him. Hold off giving him his walking papers—privately and professionally," he added. "If this lawsuit does take off, Travis is the best one to win this for you—not just because he's familiar with the case, but because he's passionate about winning it for you. And for Shawn O'Reilly," he emphasized. "Travis cares about the cases he works."

Shana hesitated. Logically, she knew Bryan was right. But she didn't know if she could handle this emotionally. She still felt raw, shaken, especially since there was a huge part of her that still loved Travis.

"I don't know," she said slowly.

"Think about it," Bryan urged, squeezing her hand before he released it. His eyes still held her in place. "That's all I ask. Just give yourself a little time to think about what I just said."

They'd been good to her. To simply brush him off seemed thankless. She supposed that he was right. Surrendering everything to Susan would dishonor her fath—her grandfather's memory. Susan *would* just spend the money recklessly and be back to where she was now. It would be just a matter of time. Shawn O'Reilly *had* taken care of her. He wasn't obligated to, but he had. She supposed she did owe the man something.

"All right," she told Bryan, "I will." Shana rose to her feet and forced a smile to her lips. "Thank you for seeing me."

"Always a pleasure," he assured her, walking her to the door.

•

Once outside Bryan's office, Shana squared her shoulders and turned toward the elevators.

Only to stop dead as she nearly walked right into Travis.

Stunned, Travis could only stare at her for a long moment. "I didn't expect to see you here."

"That makes two of us."

He seized the opportunity to reason with her again. To try to make her understand why his hands had been tied. "Shana, I couldn't tell you—"

Shana held up her hand. There was no point in going over this again. She still hurt, and it would take time for her to get over it. But she would. Eventually. "Your father's already been all through that."

"My father? What's he got to do with it?"

"I went to see him this morning to explain that I was going to be terminating your firm's—your," she amended, "services." A small, enigmatic smile came and went from her lips. "He talked me out of it. Because of the lawsuit."

Thank God for small favors, Travis thought. "Why don't we go into my office?" Travis suggested. His morning was relatively free. The first client was coming in at eleven. That left him over an hour to begin to work things out with Shana.

He began to take her arm, but she drew it away, walking ahead of him until she crossed the threshold to his office. When she did, she turned around to face him.

"Is there a lawsuit?" Shana asked in disbelief. "Is Susan really contesting the will?"

"You know her better than I do," he answered. "What do you think?"

"She was always out for herself," Shana admitted sadly, then raised her eyes to his. He saw the disappointment. "Some mother, huh?"

Gesturing to the chair before his desk, he took the other and sat down, rather than placing himself behind his desk. "Mine was running away because she couldn't handle being the mother of four boys," he told her. "If she hadn't died in the plane crash, I have a hunch she might have just kept going."

Shana sat down in the first chair. "But you had Kate."

"And you had Grace," he countered, recalling her grandmother's name.

"Yes," Shana acknowledged. And her grandmother had been wonderful. As had her grandfather, she thought ruefully. She really couldn't have asked for a better pair and she knew it. "Yes, I did. But I just really wish they had trusted me enough to tell me the truth."

"Maybe trust had nothing to do with it," Travis suggested. She looked at him quizzically. "Maybe they just didn't want to see you hurt. It's never easy, finding out that you weren't wanted by someone you believed should have wanted you on sheer principle."

"Maybe you're right," she admitted.

She sounded better, he thought. And calmer. Travis looked at her for a long moment, trying to gauge her state of mind. "So, are we okay?"

"Not yet," Shana replied honestly. "But I'm working on it."

Relief swept over him. It was going to be all right, it was just going to take time, that's all. He had a feeling he owed his father one. "I can live with that." Rising, he rounded his desk and pulled up Shawn's file. "Now, I've got an hour or so if you'd like to go over the case with me."

She had nowhere else to be and if she was alone, Shana knew her thoughts might get the better of her. Better to be busy, to have something to do, something else to think about than what had kept her awake all night. "I guess since I'm here, I might as well."

Score one for the home team, Travis thought, doing his best to suppress a relieved, triumphant grin.

"Good," he told her using his most professional tone while everything inside of him was cheering, "because we've got work to do."

Chapter 15

Shana had never been one to threaten someone in order to get her way. A civil court case was tantamount to a threat to her. It made her think of people being pitted against one another in a fight where there could be only one winner. She didn't want to go to court to get the lawsuit resolved.

Moreover, she really hated the idea that Susan was going to publicly attempt to prove that Shawn O'Reilly had essentially not been in his right mind when he changed his will.

To say that, to try to discredit and dishonor a man who had tried so many times to resolve their differences, was close to the ultimate sin as far as she was concerned. Dealing with it, with the doubts and rumors that might be raised among the people who knew her father, took a toll on her.

That, and maintaining a polite, working relationship with Travis and nothing more was taxing her to the nth degree. Especially during times when they were preparing the case, all she wanted to do was throw herself into his arms and cry. Or vent.

She didn't know how much longer she could keep it up. Or if she even wanted to. She missed the way they were.

A fortunate piece of rescheduling had them moved up on the court calendar. Suddenly, they were on the fast track and set to go in the following day.

Nerves multiplied within her even before she got the call from Travis asking her to come down to his office. She'd already been through everything several times and sincerely believed that if she was any more rehearsed, she would come across as stilted.

But she kept that to herself until she got to the office.

Travis greeted her in the hallway. Shana only got halfway through voicing her concern before Travis cut her off. He hadn't asked her down to go over the details or the testimony of the people he had lined up. All could testify that Shawn O'Reilly had been of sound mind up to and including the very moment of his death and certainly long after he'd had the revisions made to his will.

Shana didn't understand. "Then why did you call me here?" she asked. Was it to try to patch things up between them? She'd been over that dozens of times in her head, regretting her stand but not quite sure how to backtrack. Any olive branch that he would hold out at this point, she would take.

He began leading the way, not to his office but to the general conference room. "Because I thought we could still settle this out of court."

Shana stopped walking. "Are Susan and her lawyer here?"

Very gently, Travis prodded her, silently urging Shana to continue walking.

"They're in the conference room right now," he told her.

She hadn't seen Susan since the bombshell had been dropped more than a month ago. The idea of coming face-to-face with her "mother" without any warning and with only a table between them wasn't one that pleased her.

"I don't want to see her."

"You'll be seeing her in court tomorrow if we can't get this cleared up today," Travis tactfully pointed out.

Tomorrow was better than "right now." Still, she thought of the repercussions of walking into an open courtroom.

"Could we lose?"

He was honest with her. "Ninety-nine-point-nine says no. But there always is the point-one percent that says yes. It wouldn't hurt to try one last time to make Susan back off. I know you don't want your grandfather's name dragged through the mud and there's no telling what she might try as a last-ditch attempt."

It was still hard for her to accept that there was such malice within Susan. "You really think she might do something like that?"

"I do." He could see that she was wavering. "Ready?" he asked, his hand on the doorknob.

Shana took in a deep breath, bracing herself. She would have rather been anywhere else. But if she had to be here, she was glad Travis was with her.

"Ready."

For the most part, Susan's lawyer, a quiet, subdued, tall, thin man in an expensive suit and precision haircut, did most of the talking. Which surprised Shana. She wasn't accustomed to Susan holding her tongue for longer than a single heartbeat if something annoyed her.

The lawyer, Harry Wilkinson, was thoughtfully studying the latest list of character witnesses that Travis had provided him. There were more than twenty, with the promise of ten times that if the situation made it necessary.

Wilkinson raised deep brown eyes to look at Travis. "And they're all willing to swear, under oath, that Shawn O'Reilly was of sound mind?" There was no trace of emotion in his evenly modulated voice.

"Every last one of them," Travis assured him. "And they're going to blow your case out of the water."

"But I'm his only daughter."

All eyes turned toward Susan.

It was the first time that she'd spoken. The other woman's tone wasn't argumentative so much as pleading. And there was hurt in her eyes.

"I'm sure Mr. Wilkinson has already told you," Travis said patiently, "that doesn't have any bearing on the situation. Your father could have left all of his money and his restaurant to a charity dedicated to preserving gopher holes. If he was of sound mind when he made that change, there is no legal basis to contest his wishes. He was free to leave his money to whomever or whatever he wanted."

"Can he do that?" Susan demanded hotly of her lawyer. Wilkinson made no reply but his expression answered her question. "Then what do I have you for? Never mind," she snapped before he could say anything. Rising, Susan pushed back her chair along the textured carpet. "I need to get out of here." Grabbing up her purse, she hugged it as she made a beeline for the door.

"Half."

The doorknob in her hand, Susan stopped dead and then slowly turned around. She looked at the child she had never wanted, the woman whose existence now threatened her. "What?"

"Half," Shana repeated. "You can have half of everything he left to me."

"Shana—" Travis cautioned. She held her hand up to him, asking for his silence. He went along with her wishes.

Stunned, Susan walked back to the rectangular negotiations table. "Okay," she said slowly, unable to believe that it could be this easy.

"Under two conditions," Shana added once Susan was seated.

Susan blew out an angry breath. "I knew it. What're your conditions?" she demanded. "You want me to wear a hair shirt? Write you a thirty-page apology, singing your praises? What?"

Shana ignored the sarcasm. "We keep the house for six months and if one of us wants to buy the other one out at the end of that time, that's the way it'll go." They both knew that if it came to that, she would be the one doing the buying. God willing, in six months, she'd have the money to do it.

There was something more at stake here than the house where she'd grown up so badly. "What about the restaurant?"

"That's the second condition," Shana told her. She glanced toward Travis and saw admiration in his eyes. Warmth spread through her, encouraging her to go on. "We don't sell it."

"Then what's the good of having it?" Susan asked.

"Profits," Shana replied simply. "That restaurant meant a lot to your father. He'd be heartbroken if we sell it."

Susan made an impatient face. "News flash, honey, he's dead."

Shana looked at her for a long moment. "Only if you don't believe in a heaven," she answered quietly, then got back to business. "We split the profits. That's the bargain," she told her calmly, her mind made up. "If you find it unacceptable, I'll see you in court. Just remember, of the two of us, I'm a far more sympathetic plaintiff than you are," she added matter-of-factly.

Good for you. Travis was both surprised at and pleased with this new, more forceful Shana who had unexpectedly emerged.

"She's right," he said, addressing the remark to Wilkinson. And then he decided to do a preemptive strike.

"Especially if you play the 'family ties' card and the jury learns that Susan is Shana's mother. A mother who essentially abandoned her years ago. There's a lot of dirty laundry there," Travis reminded him. "And it's all on your client's side."

Temper flared in Susan's eyes, but it was clear she knew when she was outmaneuvered. "You win," Susan snapped angrily. "Again. You *always* win," she lamented, her voice momentarily cracking.

"It was never about winning and losing, Susan," she said. Shana'd decided that the word "mother" sounded too foreign to her ear. "Never," she emphasized.

Susan glared at her. "Then what was it about?"

"About being a family," Travis interjected. Both women looked at him. "The way Shawn and his wife wanted you to be. If you couldn't take responsibility for her as her mother, then they wanted you to at least be the sister she needed in her corner. They wanted you to be part of the unit. Both of you," he emphasized, looking from one to the other.

"Pretty speech, lawyer-boy. She paying you by the word?" Not waiting for him to give her an answer, Susan snorted, dismissing what he'd just said. "They didn't want me to be part of anything. They were all only too happy when I left."

This time it was Shana who contradicted Susan.

"If it looked that way to you, it was only because you kept insisting on hurting them. Every time they saw you in an abusive relationship, it hurt them," Shana insisted when Susan seemed unconvinced. "Dad even wanted to try an intervention. That was just before you ran off with that band roadie. He felt guilty that he waited too long and missed the opportunity to try to turn you around." It hurt her just to think about how much that affected the man. "It bothered him for years."

Susan opened her mouth to make another retort, then closed it again. There was an odd expression on her face, as if, after all the thousands of words that had been hurled at her, she was finally hearing them for the first time.

And then, as if collecting herself, Susan waved her hand, dismissing everything. "You win. I'll drop the lawsuit."

Inwardly, Shana breathed a sigh of relief. "I meant what I said about half of everything," she said out loud to Susan.

"Yeah, we'll talk." But this time, it didn't sound as if Susan was just shining her on the way she normally did. Looking at her lawyer, Susan tucked her arm through his, urging him to his feet. "Let's go, Harry."

"Yes, we'll talk," Shana echoed, calling after her as Susan left the room.

Was it her imagination, or had Susan's lawyer blushed just a tad when Susan had threaded her arm through his to hurry him along?

Susan and Wilkinson? If only. The man seemed to have a calming influence on Susan and heaven knew that the woman was in desperate need of that. As well as a strong, even hand.

Maybe miracles did happen.

"Well, looks like it's over," Travis said, finally breaking the silence. "You won," In more ways than one, he added silently. "This means you won't have to go to court."

Shana took in a long breath to steady herself. She hadn't realized that she was trembling inside until just now. "It's really over?" she heard herself asking incredulously.

He smiled at her. "Yes, it's really over."

Over.

Was *everything* over? Shana paused for a moment before speaking, searching for the right words—if things like that existed in this case—even as she wondered if she actually *should* say anything.

And then she raised her eyes to his. If she didn't ask now, she never would. And she'd probably regret it for the rest of her life. She'd seen enough regrets. She didn't want to be shackled by them.

"Is it over between us?"

Travis stopped gathering his papers together and looked at her. It took him a moment to answer. A moment in which his heart just ceased beating altogether. He chose his words carefully, knowing the wrong ones could ruin everything. "That's for you to decide."

"You have no input in this?" She tried hard not to sound as disappointed as she felt. She was wrong, wasn't she? He didn't care. Not anymore. And that was her doing.

His words were measured out evenly, as if he'd paused to make sure that they were all equally crafted. "You know the answer to that. But I won't force you, if that's what you're asking."

She'd lost something precious before she even

realized she had it, didn't she? "I'm asking if you care which way I decide."

"If I care?" he asked incredulously, looking at her as if she'd just lost her mind. "If I care? Damn it, Shana, I care so much, I'm amazed it's not spilling out of every pore. It's everything I can do not to have set siege to your house, not to have barged in and *made* you forgive me."

A sad expression played along his face. "But it doesn't work that way and I know it. You can't make anyone feel what they don't want to feel." How could she not know that every day was an exercise in restraint? That he still loved her so much that it ripped him up inside to interact with her and pretend otherwise. "You just hope to God that there's a miracle in the offing with your name on it."

"A miracle?" Shana echoed. The miracle was that she cared. That she loved. That she could still love after what she'd just endured. "I don't know about a miracle, but I do know that I'd like to give us another try." She took a breath, afraid that if she hesitated for a moment, she'd lose her nerve. "I've missed you something awful, Travis. And I hate being just a client."

Travis smiled and shook his head. "You were never just a client, Shana. You couldn't be." He threaded his fingers through her hair, his eyes already making love to her. "I'm a very down-to-earth kind of guy. Ask anyone here and they'll all tell you the same thing. Including my family. But the first time I saw you, the earth moved.

"It stopped moving the day I thought I lost you. And working with you these last few weeks, knowing I couldn't have you," because he wouldn't presume to forcibly make her change her mind, "was absolutely hell on earth. I love you, Shana. Whether or not you want to be with me doesn't change that. I love you. I have from the first moment I saw you. I will until the day I die." He paused, letting his words sink in, searching her face to see if they'd had any effect. "Does that answer your question?"

She smiled at him and shook her head, not in response but in amazement. "You are a lawyer," she said. Then, because he looked at her quizzically, she added, "Explaining everything down to the bottom line and then some."

"I want to make sure that there's no room for misinterpretation." He framed her face with his hands, wanting to kiss her so badly, he thought he would explode. "Or doubt."

"Is it my turn now?" she asked.

Only if you say the right thing. He inclined his head. "If you like."

Here went everything, she thought. "I love you."

Travis waited for more. But she stood there, her lips pressed together, looking at him hopefully.

"That's it?" he asked.

"That's it," she echoed, then, because she'd just laid her heart at his feet, Shana added, "That's everything."

"Yes," he agreed, sliding his hands from her face down her shoulders to her waist. He took her into his arms. "That certainly is."

Then, because he couldn't hold back any longer, Travis brought his mouth down to hers, losing himself in the kiss that had haunted his dreams all these nights he'd spent away from her. Absence had showed him all too acutely that he was no good without her. And there was only one cure for that.

The sound of a short rap on the door forced them to terminate the kiss but not to pull apart. Not yet.

Looking toward the door, Travis saw his father popping his head in.

One look told Bryan all he needed to know. A feeling of deep satisfaction pervaded him. Kate was going to be absolutely thrilled, he thought. Christmas was going to be a mob scene this year.

He glanced at his watch, doing a quick calculation before saying, "You two can have the conference room for the next hour. But I don't think I can hold the others off longer than that."

Without waiting for a response, Bryan winked and then firmly closed the door behind him.

She should be uneasy, Shana thought. But all she felt was happy. So very happy. She glanced from the door to Travis.

"Just what is it that your father thinks we're going to be doing in here?" The man didn't think they were going to make love in here, did he? Heaven help her, she did like the idea.

Travis had a pretty good idea he knew what his father was thinking. "Proposing comes to mind."

It took everything she had not to let her slackened jaw drop. Nothing worse than looking like a gapping, brainless woman. "Excuse me, but I think my hearing just failed. I thought you just said 'proposing.'"

He was still holding her in his arms and right now, he didn't think that he was ever going to release her. Or at least, not any time soon. "I did."

Was she dreaming? Or was this really happening, even after the way she'd treated him. "To me?"

He pretended to look around. "You see anyone else in here?"

How could a man look innocent and incredibly sexy at the same time? "No," she breathed.

He pressed a kiss to her left temple and then to her right one. His breath whispered along her skin as he said, "Then I guess you get me by default."

"*Fault,*" she said, picking up on the last part of the word, "has absolutely nothing to do with it," Shana assured him. Rising up, she pressed her body against his as she tightening her arms around his neck. Her own body heated up several degrees.

He looked into her face. "Are you saying yes?"

She cocked her head. "Give me ten minutes to play hard-to-get first."

He brushed a soft, quick kiss against her lips. "I'll give you twenty if you like."

Her heart was already hammering hard. "No, ten'll be more than enough."

He laughed, just before he kissed her again with feeling.

Ten minutes turned out to be much too long. "Yes!" Shana cried within ten seconds, just before she threw herself completely into the kiss she pressed against his lips.

* * * * *

*Celebrate 60 years of pure reading
pleasure with Harlequin®!
Silhouette® Romantic Suspense is celebrating
with the glamour-filled, adrenaline-charged series
LOVE IN 60 SECONDS
starting in April 2009.
Six stories that promise to bring the glitz
of Las Vegas, the danger of revenge,
the mystery of a missing diamond,
family scandals and ripped-from-the-headlines
intrigue. Get your heart racing as love
happens in sixty seconds!*

Enjoy a sneak peek of
USA TODAY *bestselling author
Marie Ferrarella's*
*THE HEIRESS'S 2-WEEK AFFAIR
Available April 2009
from Silhouette® Romantic Suspense.*

Eight years ago Matt Shaffer had vanished out of Natalie Rothchild's life, leaving behind a one-line note tucked under a pillow that had grown cold: *I'm sorry, but this just isn't going to work.*

That was it. No explanation, no real indication of remorse. The note had been as clinical and compassionless as an eviction notice, which, in effect, it had been, Natalie thought as she navigated through the morning traffic. Matt had written the note to evict her from his life.

She'd spent the next two weeks crying, breaking down without warning as she walked down the street, or as she sat staring at a meal she couldn't bring herself to eat.

Candace, she remembered with a bittersweet pang, had tried to get her to go clubbing in order to get her to forget about Matt.

She'd turned her twin down, but she did get her act together. If Matt didn't think enough of their relationship to try to contact her, to try to make her understand why he'd changed so radically from lover to stranger, then to hell with him. He was dead to her, she resolved. And he'd remained that way.

Until twenty minutes ago.

The adrenaline in her veins kept mounting.

Natalie focused on her driving. Vegas in the daylight wasn't nearly as alluring, as magical and glitzy as it was after dark. Like an aging woman best seen in soft lighting, Vegas's imperfections were all visible in the daylight. Natalie supposed that was why people like her sister didn't like to get up until noon. They lived for the night.

Except that Candace could no longer do that.

The thought brought a fresh, sharp ache with it.

"Damn it, Candy, what a waste," Natalie murmured under her breath.

She pulled up before the Janus casino. One of the three valets currently on duty came to life and made a beeline for her vehicle.

"Welcome to the Janus," the young attendant said cheerfully as he opened her door with a flourish.

"We'll see," she replied solemnly.

As he pulled away with her car, Natalie looked up at the casino's logo. Janus was the Roman god with two faces, one pointed toward the past, the other facing the future. It struck her as rather ironic, given what she was doing here, seeking out someone from her past in order to get answers so that the future could be settled.

The moment she entered the casino, the Vegas phenomena took hold. It was like stepping into a world where time did not matter or even make an appearance. There was only a sense of "now."

Because in Natalie's experience she'd discovered that bartenders knew the inner workings of any establishment they worked for better than anyone else, she made her way to the first bar she saw within the casino.

The bartender in attendance was a gregarious man in his early forties. He had a quick, sexy smile, which was probably one of the main reasons he'd been hired. His name tag identified him as Kevin.

Moving to her end of the bar, Kevin asked, "What'll it be, pretty lady?"

"Information." She saw a dubious look cross his brow. To counter that, she took out her badge. Granted she wasn't here in an official capacity, but Kevin didn't need to know that. "Were you on duty last night?"

Kevin began to wipe the gleaming black surface of the bar. "You mean during the gala?"

"Yes."

The smile gracing his lips was a satisfied one. Last night had obviously been profitable for him, she judged. "I caught an extra shift."

She took out Candace's photograph and carefully

placed it on the bar. "Did you happen to see this woman there?"

The bartender glanced at the picture. Mild interest turned to recognition. "You mean Candace Rothchild? Yeah, she was here, loud and brassy as always. But not for long," he added, looking rather disappointed. There was always a circus when Candace was around, Natalie thought. "She and the boss had at it and then he had our head of security escort her out."

She latched onto the first part of his statement. "They argued? About what?"

He shook his head. "Couldn't tell you. Too far away for anything but body language," he confessed.

"And the head of security?" she asked.

"He got her to leave."

She leaned in over the bar. "Tell me about him."

"Don't know much," the bartender admitted. "Just that his name's Matt Shaffer. Boss flew him in from L.A., where he was head of security for Montgomery Enterprises."

There was no avoiding it, she thought darkly. She was going to have to talk to Matt. The thought left her cold. "Do you know where I can find him right now?"

Kevin glanced at his watch. "He should be in his office. On the second floor, toward the rear." He gave her the numbers of the rooms where the monitors that kept watch over the casino guests as they tried their luck against the house were located.

Taking out a twenty, she placed it on the bar. "Thanks for your help."

Kevin slipped the bill into his vest pocket. "Any time, lovely lady," he called after her. "Any time."

She debated going up the stairs, then decided on the elevator. The car that took her up to the second floor was empty. Natalie stepped out of the elevator, looked around to get her bearings and then walked toward the rear of the floor.

"Into the Valley of Death rode the six hundred," she silently recited, digging deep for a line from a poem by Tennyson. Wrapping her hand around a brass handle, she opened one of the glass doors and walked in.

The woman whose desk was closest to the door looked up. "You can't come in here. This is a restricted area."

Natalie already had her ID in her hand and held it up. "I'm looking for Matt Shaffer," she told the woman.

God, even saying his name made her mouth go dry. She was supposed to be over him, to have moved on with her life. What happened?

The woman began to answer her. "He's—"

"Right here."

The deep voice came from behind her. Natalie felt every single nerve ending go on tactical alert at the same moment that all the hairs at the back of her neck stood up. Eight years had passed, but she would have recognized his voice anywhere.

* * * * *

*Why did Matt Shaffer leave
heiress-turned-cop Natalie Rothchild?
What does he know about the death
of Natalie's twin sister?
Come and meet these two reunited lovers and learn
the secrets of the Rothchild family in
THE HEIRESS'S 2-WEEK AFFAIR
by USA TODAY bestselling author
Marie Ferrarella.
The first book in Silhouette® Romantic Suspense's
wildly romantic new continuity,
LOVE IN 60 SECONDS!
Available April 2009.*

CELEBRATE
60 YEARS
OF PURE READING PLEASURE
WITH **HARLEQUIN**®!

Look for Silhouette®
Romantic Suspense in April!

Love In 60 Seconds

Bright lights. Big city. Hearts in overdrive.

Silhouette® Romantic Suspense is celebrating
Harlequin's 60th Anniversary with six stories that
promise to bring readers the glitz of Las Vegas,
the danger of revenge, the mystery of a missing
diamond, and family scandals.

**Look for the first title, *The Heiress's 2-Week Affair*
by *USA TODAY* bestselling author
Marie Ferrarella, on sale in April!**

His 7-Day Fiancée by **Gail Barrett**	May
The 9-Month Bodyguard by **Cindy Dees**	June
Prince Charming for 1 Night by **Nina Bruhns**	July
Her 24-Hour Protector by **Loreth Anne White**	August
5 minutes to Marriage by **Carla Cassidy**	September

You're invited to join our Tell Harlequin Reader Panel!

By joining our new reader panel you will:

- Receive Harlequin® books—they are FREE and yours to keep with no obligation to purchase anything!
- Participate in fun online surveys
- Exchange opinions and ideas with women just like you
- Have a say in our new book ideas and help us publish the best in women's fiction

In addition, you will have a chance to win great prizes and receive special gifts! See Web site for details. Some conditions apply. Space is limited.

To join, visit us at
www.TellHarlequin.com.

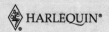

REQUEST YOUR FREE BOOKS!

2 FREE NOVELS PLUS 2 FREE GIFTS!

SPECIAL EDITION®

Life, Love and Family!

The Inside Romance newsletter has a NEW look for the new year!

Same great content, brand-new look!

The Inside Romance newsletter is a FREE quarterly newsletter highlighting our upcoming series releases and promotions!

Click on the Inside Romance link on the front page of **www.eHarlequin.com** or e-mail us at insideromance@harlequin.ca to sign up to receive your FREE newsletter today!

You can also subscribe by writing to us at: HARLEQUIN BOOKS Attention: Customer Service Department P.O. Box 9057, Buffalo, NY 14269-9057

Please allow 4-6 weeks for delivery of the first issue by mail.

IRNNEW09

Silhouette®

COMING NEXT MONTH
Available March 31, 2009

#1963 THE BRAVO BACHELOR—Christine Rimmer
Bravo Family Ties
For attorney Gabe Bravo, sweet-talking young widow
Mary Hofstetter into selling her ranch to BravoCorp should have
been a cinch. But the stubborn mom turned the tables and got him
to bargain away his bachelorhood instead!

#1964 A REAL LIVE COWBOY—Judy Duarte
Fortunes of Texas: Return to Red Rock
CEO William "J.R." Fortune gave up the L.A. fast life to pursue
his dream of becoming a Texas rancher. Luckily, hiring decorator
and Red Rock native Isabella Mendoza to spruce up his new spread
ensured he'd get a very warm welcome in his brand-new life!

#1965 A WEAVER WEDDING—Allison Leigh
Famous Families
A one-night stand with Axel Clay left Tara Browning pregnant.
But when she was forced to share very close quarters with the sexy
bodyguard, would she end up with a love to last a lifetime?

#1966 HEALING THE M.D.'S HEART—Nicole Foster
The Brothers of Rancho Pintada
To help his sick son, Duran Forrester would do anything—including
a road trip to Rancho Pintada to find the long-lost family who might
hold the key to a cure. But first, he crossed paths with pediatrician
Lia Kerrigan, who had a little TLC for father and son alike....

#1967 THE RANCHER & THE RELUCTANT PRINCESS—Christine Flynn
After her unscripted remarks blew up in the tabloids, Princess Sophie
of Valdovia needed to cool off out of the public eye in middle-of-
nowhere Montana. But that's where things heated up—royally—with
rancher and single dad Carter McLeod....

#1968 THE FAMILY HE WANTED—Karen Sandler
Fostering Family
Bestselling novelist Sam Harrison had it all—so why did the former
foster kid-made-good feel so empty inside? The answer came when
old friend Jana McPartland showed up on his porch, pregnant and in
distress, and he realized that it was family he wanted...and family he
was about to find.

SPECIAL EDITION